Grim Tales

Grim Tales

Edith Nesbit

MINT EDITIONS

Grim Tales was first published in 1893.

This edition published by Mint Editions 2020.

ISBN 9781513269801 | E-ISBN 9781513274805

Published by Mint Editions®

MINT
EDITIONS
minteditionbooks.com

Publishing Director: Jennifer Newens
Design & Production: Rachel Lopez Metzger
Typesetting: Westchester Publishing Services

Contents

THE EBONY FRAME

To be rich is a luxurious sensation—the more so when you have plumbed the depths of hard-up-ness as a Fleet Street hack, a picker-up of unconsidered pars, a reporter, an unappreciated journalist— all callings utterly inconsistent with one's family feeling and one's direct descent from the Dukes of Picardy.

When my Aunt Dorcas died and left me seven hundred a year and a furnished house in Chelsea, I felt that life had nothing left to offer except immediate possession of the legacy. Even Mildred Mayhew, whom I had hitherto regarded as my life's light, became less luminous. I was not engaged to Mildred, but I lodged with her mother, and I sang duets with Mildred, and gave her gloves when it would run to it, which was seldom. She was a dear good girl, and I meant to marry her some day. It is very nice to feel that a good little woman is thinking of you—it helps you in your work—and it is pleasant to know she will say "Yes" when you say "Will you?"

But, as I say, my legacy almost put Mildred out of my head, especially as she was staying with friends in the country just then.

Before the first gloss was off my new mourning I was seated in my aunt's own armchair in front of the fire in the dining-room of my own house. My own house! It was grand, but rather lonely. I *did* think of Mildred just then.

The room was comfortably furnished with oak and leather. On the walls hung a few fairly good oil-paintings, but the space above the mantelpiece was disfigured by an exceedingly bad print, "The Trial of Lord William Russell," framed in a dark frame. I got up to look at it. I had visited my aunt with dutiful regularity, but I never remembered seeing this frame before. It was not intended for a print, but for an oil-painting. It was of fine ebony, beautifully and curiously carved.

I looked at it with growing interest, and when my aunt's housemaid—I had retained her modest staff of servants—came in with the lamp, I asked her how long the print had been there.

"Mistress only bought it two days afore she was took ill," she said; "but the frame—she didn't want to buy a new one—so she got this out of the attic. There's lots of curious old things there, sir."

"Had my aunt had this frame long?"

"Oh yes, sir. It come long afore I did, and I've been here seven years come Christmas. There was a picture in it—that's upstairs too—but it's that black and ugly it might as well be a chimley-back."

I felt a desire to see this picture. What if it were some priceless old master in which my aunt's eyes had only seen rubbish?

Directly after breakfast next morning I paid a visit to the lumber-room.

It was crammed with old furniture enough to stock a curiosity shop. All the house was furnished solidly in the early Victorian style, and in this room everything not in keeping with the "drawing-room suite" ideal was stowed away. Tables of papier-maché and mother-of-pearl, straight-backed chairs with twisted feet and faded needlework cushions, firescreens of old-world design, oak bureaux with brass handles, a little work-table with its faded moth-eaten silk flutings hanging in disconsolate shreds: on these and the dust that covered them blazed the full daylight as I drew up the blinds. I promised myself a good time in re-enshrining these household gods in my parlour, and promoting the Victorian suite to the attic. But at present my business was to find the picture as "black as the chimley-back;" and presently, behind a heap of hideous still-life studies, I found it.

Jane the housemaid identified it at once. I took it downstairs carefully and examined it. No subject, no colour were distinguishable. There was a splodge of a darker tint in the middle, but whether it was figure or tree or house no man could have told. It seemed to be painted on a very thick panel bound with leather. I decided to send it to one of those persons who pour on rotting family portraits the water of eternal youth—mere soap and water Mr. Besant tells us it is; but even as I did so the thought occurred to me to try my own restorative hand at a corner of it.

My bath-sponge, soap, and nailbrush vigorously applied for a few seconds showed me that there was no picture to clean! Bare oak presented itself to my persevering brush. I tried the other side, Jane watching me with indulgent interest. The same result. Then the truth dawned on me. Why was the panel so thick? I tore off the leather binding, and the panel divided and fell to the ground in a cloud of dust. There were two pictures—they had been nailed face to face. I leaned them against the wall, and the next moment I was leaning against it myself.

For one of the pictures was myself—a perfect portrait—no shade of expression or turn of feature wanting. Myself—in a cavalier dress, "love-locks and all!" When had this been done? And how, without my knowledge? Was this some whim of my aunt's?

"Lor', sir!" the shrill surprise of Jane at my elbow; "what a lovely photo it is! Was it a fancy ball, sir?"

"Yes," I stammered. "I—I don't think I want anything more now. You can go."

She went; and I turned, still with my heart beating violently, to the other picture. This was a woman of the type of beauty beloved of Burne Jones and Rossetti—straight nose, low brows, full lips, thin hands, large deep luminous eyes. She wore a black velvet gown. It was a full-length portrait. Her arms rested on a table beside her, and her head on her hands; but her face was turned full forward, and her eyes met those of the spectator bewilderingly. On the table by her were compasses and instruments whose uses I did not know, books, a goblet, and a miscellaneous heap of papers and pens. I saw all this afterwards. I believe it was a quarter of an hour before I could turn my eyes away from hers. I have never seen any other eyes like hers. They appealed, as a child's or a dog's do; they commanded, as might those of an empress.

"Shall I sweep up the dust, sir?" Curiosity had brought Jane back. I acceded. I turned from her my portrait. I kept between her and the woman in the black velvet. When I was alone again I tore down "The Trial of Lord William Russell," and I put the picture of the woman in its strong ebony frame.

Then I wrote to a frame-maker for a frame for my portrait. It had so long lived face to face with this beautiful witch that I had not the heart to banish it from her presence; from which, it will be perceived that I am by nature a somewhat sentimental person.

The new frame came home, and I hung it opposite the fireplace. An exhaustive search among my aunt's papers showed no explanation of the portrait of myself, no history of the portrait of the woman with the wonderful eyes. I only learned that all the old furniture together had come to my aunt at the death of my great-uncle, the head of the family; and I should have concluded that the resemblance was only a family one, if every one who came in had not exclaimed at the "speaking likeness." I adopted Jane's "fancy ball" explanation.

And there, one might suppose, the matter of the portraits ended. One might suppose it, that is, if there were not evidently a good deal more written here about it. However, to me, then, the matter seemed ended.

I went to see Mildred; I invited her and her mother to come and stay with me. I rather avoided glancing at the picture in the ebony frame. I could not forget, nor remember without singular emotion, the look in the eyes of that woman when mine first met them. I shrank from meeting that look again.

I reorganized the house somewhat, preparing for Mildred's visit. I turned the dining-room into a drawing-room. I brought down much of the old-fashioned furniture, and, after a long day of arranging and re-arranging, I sat down before the fire, and, lying back in a pleasant languor, I idly raised my eyes to the picture. I met her dark, deep hazel eyes, and once more my gaze was held fixed as by a strong magic—the kind of fascination that keeps one sometimes staring for whole minutes into one's own eyes in the glass. I gazed into her eyes, and felt my own dilate, pricked with a smart like the smart of tears.

"I wish," I said, "oh, how I wish you were a woman, and not a picture! Come down! Ah, come down!"

I laughed at myself as I spoke; but even as I laughed I held out my arms.

I was not sleepy; I was not drunk. I was as wide awake and as sober as ever was a man in this world. And yet, as I held out my arms, I saw the eyes of the picture dilate, her lips tremble—if I were to be hanged for saying it, it is true. Her hands moved slightly, and a sort of flicker of a smile passed over her face.

I sprang to my feet. "This won't do," I said, still aloud. "Firelight does play strange tricks. I'll have the lamp."

I pulled myself together and made for the bell. My hand was on it, when I heard a sound behind me, and turned—the bell still unrung. The fire had burned low, and the corners of the room were deeply shadowed; but, surely, there—behind the tall worked chair—was something darker than a shadow.

"I must face this out," I said, "or I shall never be able to face myself again." I left the bell, I seized the poker, and battered the dull coals to a blaze. Then I stepped back resolutely, and looked up at the picture. The ebony frame was empty! From the shadow of the worked chair came a silken rustle, and out of the shadow the woman of the picture was coming—coming towards me.

I hope I shall never again know a moment of terror so blank and absolute. I could not have moved or spoken to save my life. Either all the known laws of nature were nothing, or I was mad. I stood trembling, but, I am thankful to remember, I stood still, while the black velvet gown swept across the hearthrug towards me.

Next moment a hand touched me—a hand soft, warm, and human—and a low voice said, "You called me. I am here."

At that touch and that voice the world seemed to give a sort of bewildering half-turn. I hardly know how to express it, but at once it seemed not awful—not even unusual—for portraits to become flesh—only most natural, most right, most unspeakably fortunate.

I laid my hand on hers. I looked from her to my portrait. I could not see it in the firelight.

"We are not strangers," I said.

"Oh no, not strangers." Those luminous eyes were looking up into mine—those red lips were near me. With a passionate cry—a sense of having suddenly recovered life's one great good, that had seemed wholly lost—I clasped her in my arms. She was no ghost—she was a woman—the only woman in the world.

"How long," I said, "O love—how long since I lost you?"

She leaned back, hanging her full weight on the hands that were clasped behind my head.

"How can I tell how long? There is no time in hell," she answered.

It was not a dream. Ah, no—there are no such dreams. I wish to God there could be. When in dreams do I see her eyes, hear her voice, feel her lips against my cheek, hold her hands to my lips, as I did that night—the supreme night of my life? At first we hardly spoke. It seemed enough—

". . . after long grief and pain,
To feel the arms of my true love
Round me once again."

It is very difficult to tell this story. There are no words to express the sense of glad reunion, the complete realization of every hope and dream of a life, that came upon me as I sat with my hand in hers and looked into her eyes.

How could it have been a dream, when I left her sitting in the straight-backed chair, and went down to the kitchen to tell the maids I should want nothing more—that I was busy, and did not wish to be disturbed; when I fetched wood for the fire with my own hands, and, bringing it in, found her still sitting there—saw the little brown head turn as I entered, saw the love in her dear eyes; when I threw myself at her feet and blessed the day I was born, since life had given me this?

Not a thought of Mildred: all the other things in my life were a dream—this, its one splendid reality.

"I am wondering," she said after a while, when we had made such cheer each of the other as true lovers may after long parting—"I am wondering how much you remember of our past."

"I remember nothing," I said. "Oh, my dear lady, my dear sweetheart—I remember nothing but that I love you—that I have loved you all my life."

"You remember nothing—really nothing?"

"Only that I am yours; that we have both suffered; that—Tell me, my mistress dear, all that you remember. Explain it all to me. Make me understand. And yet—No, I don't want to understand. It is enough that we are together."

If it was a dream, why have I never dreamed it again?

She leaned down towards me, her arm lay on my neck, and drew my head till it rested on her shoulder. "I am a ghost, I suppose," she said, laughing softly; and her laughter stirred memories which I just grasped at, and just missed. "But you and I know better, don't we? I will tell you everything you have forgotten. We loved each other—ah! no, you have not forgotten that—and when you came back from the war we were to be married. Our pictures were painted before you went away. You know I was more learned than women of that day. Dear one, when you were gone they said I was a witch. They tried me. They said I should be burned. Just because I had looked at the stars and had gained more knowledge than they, they must needs bind me to a stake and let me be eaten by the fire. And you far away!"

Her whole body trembled and shrank. O love, what dream would have told me that my kisses would soothe even that memory?

"The night before," she went on, "the devil did come to me. I was innocent before—you know it, don't you? And even then my sin was for you—for you—because of the exceeding love I bore you. The devil came, and I sold my soul to eternal flame. But I got a good price. I got the right to come back, through my picture (if any one looking at it wished for me), as long as my picture stayed in its ebony frame. That frame was not carved by man's hand. I got the right to come back to you. Oh, my heart's heart, and another thing I won, which you shall hear anon. They burned me for a witch, they made me suffer hell on earth. Those faces, all crowding round, the crackling wood and the smell of the smoke—"

"O love! no more—no more."

"When my mother sat that night before my picture she wept, and cried, 'Come back, my poor lost child!' And I went to her, with glad leaps of heart. Dear, she shrank from me, she fled, she shrieked and moaned of ghosts. She had our pictures covered from sight and put again in the ebony frame. She had promised me my picture should stay always there. Ah, through all these years your face was against mine."

She paused.

"But the man you loved?"

"You came home. My picture was gone. They lied to you, and you married another woman; but some day I knew you would walk the world again and that I should find you."

"The other gain?" I asked.

"The other gain," she said slowly, "I gave my soul for. It is this. If you also will give up your hopes of heaven I can remain a woman, I can move in your world—I can be your wife. Oh, my dear, after all these years, at last—at last."

"If I sacrifice my soul," I said slowly, with no thought of the imbecility of such talk in our "so-called nineteenth century"—"if I sacrifice my soul, I win you? Why, love, it's a contradiction in terms. You *are* my soul."

Her eyes looked straight into mine. Whatever might happen, whatever did happen, whatever may happen, our two souls in that moment met, and became one.

"Then you choose—you deliberately choose—to give up your hopes of heaven for me, as I gave up mine for you?"

"I decline," I said, "to give up my hope of heaven on any terms. Tell me what I must do, that you and I may make our heaven here—as now, my dear love."

"I will tell you to-morrow," she said. "Be alone here to-morrow night—twelve is ghost's time, isn't it?—and then I will come out of the picture and never go back to it. I shall live with you, and die, and be buried, and there will be an end of me. But we shall live first, my heart's heart."

I laid my head on her knee. A strange drowsiness overcame me. Holding her hand against my cheek, I lost consciousness. When I awoke the grey November dawn was glimmering, ghost-like, through the uncurtained window. My head was pillowed on my arm, which rested—I raised my head quickly—ah! not on my lady's knee, but on the needle-worked cushion of the straight-backed chair. I sprang to my feet. I was stiff with cold, and dazed with dreams, but I turned my eyes on the picture. There she sat, my lady, my dear love. I held out my arms, but the passionate cry I would have uttered died on my lips. She had said twelve o'clock. Her lightest word was my law. So I only stood in front of the picture and gazed into those grey-green eyes till tears of passionate happiness filled my own.

"Oh, my dear, my dear, how shall I pass the hours till I hold you again?"

No thought, then, of my whole life's completion and consummation being a dream.

I staggered up to my room, fell across my bed, and slept heavily and dreamlessly. When I awoke it was high noon. Mildred and her mother were coming to lunch.

I remembered, at one shock, Mildred's coming and her existence.

Now, indeed, the dream began.

With a penetrating sense of the futility of any action apart from *her*, I gave the necessary orders for the reception of my guests. When Mildred and her mother came I received them with cordiality; but my genial phrases all seemed to be some one else's. My voice sounded like an echo; my heart was other where.

Still, the situation was not intolerable until the hour when afternoon tea was served in the drawing-room. Mildred and her mother kept the conversational pot boiling with a profusion of genteel commonplaces, and I bore it, as one can bear mild purgatories when one is in sight of heaven. I looked up at my sweetheart in the ebony frame, and I felt that anything that might happen, any irresponsible imbecility, any bathos of boredom, was nothing, if, after it all, *she* came to me again.

And yet, when Mildred, too, looked at the portrait, and said, "What a fine lady! One of your flames, Mr. Devigne?" I had a sickening sense of impotent irritation, which became absolute torture when Mildred—how could I ever have admired that chocolate-box barmaid style of prettiness?—threw herself into the high-backed chair, covering the needlework with her ridiculous flounces, and added, "Silence gives consent! Who is it, Mr. Devigne? Tell us all about her: I am sure she has a story."

Poor little Mildred, sitting there smiling, serene in her confidence that her every word charmed me—sitting there with her rather pinched waist, her rather tight boots, her rather vulgar voice—sitting in the chair where my dear lady had sat when she told me her story! I could not bear it.

"Don't sit there," I said; "it's not comfortable!"

But the girl would not be warned. With a laugh that set every nerve in my body vibrating with annoyance, she said, "Oh, dear! mustn't I even sit in the same chair as your black-velvet woman?"

I looked at the chair in the picture. It *was* the same; and in her chair Mildred was sitting. Then a horrible sense of the reality of Mildred came upon me. Was all this a reality after all? But for fortunate chance might Mildred have occupied, not only her chair, but her place in my life? I rose.

"I hope you won't think me very rude," I said; "but I am obliged to go out."

I forget what appointment I alleged. The lie came readily enough.

I faced Mildred's pouts with the hope that she and her mother would not wait dinner for me. I fled. In another minute I was safe, alone, under the chill, cloudy autumn sky—free to think, think, think of my dear lady.

I walked for hours along streets and squares; I lived over again and again every look, word, and hand-touch—every kiss; I was completely, unspeakably happy.

Mildred was utterly forgotten: my lady of the ebony frame filled my heart and soul and spirit.

As I heard eleven boom through the fog, I turned, and went home.

When I got to my street, I found a crowd surging through it, a strong red light filling the air.

A house was on fire. Mine.

I elbowed my way through the crowd.

The picture of my lady—that, at least, I could save!

As I sprang up the steps, I saw, as in a dream—yes, all this was *really* dream-like—I saw Mildred leaning out of the first-floor window, wringing her hands.

"Come back, sir," cried a fireman; "we'll get the young lady out right enough."

But *my* lady? I went on up the stairs, cracking, smoking, and as hot as hell, to the room where her picture was. Strange to say, I only felt that the picture was a thing we should like to look on through the long glad wedded life that was to be ours. I never thought of it as being one with her.

As I reached the first floor I felt arms round my neck. The smoke was too thick for me to distinguish features.

"Save me!" a voice whispered. I clasped a figure in my arms, and, with a strange dis-ease, bore it down the shaking stairs and out into safety. It was Mildred. I knew *that* directly I clasped her.

"Stand back," cried the crowd.

"Every one's safe," cried a fireman.

The flames leaped from every window. The sky grew redder and redder. I sprang from the hands that would have held me. I leaped up the steps. I crawled up the stairs. Suddenly the whole horror of the situation came on me. *"As long as my picture remains in the ebony frame."* What if picture and frame perished together?

I fought with the fire, and with my own choking inability to fight with it. I pushed on. I must save my picture. I reached the drawing-room.

As I sprang in I saw my lady—I swear it—through the smoke and the flames, hold out her arms to me—to me—who came too late to save her, and to save my own life's joy. I never saw her again.

Before I could reach her, or cry out to her, I felt the floor yield beneath my feet, and I fell into the fiery hell below.

How did they save me? What does that matter? They saved me somehow—curse them. Every stick of my aunt's furniture was destroyed. My friends pointed out that, as the furniture was heavily insured, the carelessness of a nightly-studious housemaid had done me no harm.

No harm!

That was how I won and lost my only love.

I deny, with all my soul in the denial, that it was a dream. There are no such dreams. Dreams of longing and pain there are in plenty, but dreams of complete, of unspeakable happiness—ah, no—it is the rest of life that is the dream.

But if I think that, why have I married Mildred, and grown stout and dull and prosperous?

I tell you it is all *this* that is the dream; my dear lady only is the reality. And what does it matter what one does in a dream?

JOHN CHARRINGTON'S WEDDING

No one ever thought that May Forster would marry John Charrington; but he thought differently, and things which John Charrington intended had a queer way of coming to pass. He asked her to marry him before he went up to Oxford. She laughed and refused him. He asked her again next time he came home. Again she laughed, tossed her dainty blonde head, and again refused. A third time he asked her; she said it was becoming a confirmed bad habit, and laughed at him more than ever.

John was not the only man who wanted to marry her: she was the belle of our village *coterie*, and we were all in love with her more or less; it was a sort of fashion, like heliotrope ties or Inverness capes. Therefore we were as much annoyed as surprised when John Charrington walked into our little local Club—we held it in a loft over the saddler's, I remember—and invited us all to his wedding.

"Your wedding?"

"You don't mean it?"

"Who's the happy fair? When's it to be?"

John Charrington filled his pipe and lighted it before he replied. Then he said—

"I'm sorry to deprive you fellows of your only joke—but Miss Forster and I are to be married in September."

"You don't mean it?"

"He's got the mitten again, and it's turned his head."

"No," I said, rising, "I see it's true. Lend me a pistol some one—or a first-class fare to the other end of Nowhere. Charrington has bewitched the only pretty girl in our twenty-mile radius. Was it mesmerism, or a love-potion, Jack?"

"Neither, sir, but a gift you'll never have—perseverance—and the best luck a man ever had in this world."

There was something in his voice that silenced me, and all chaff of the other fellows failed to draw him further.

The queer thing about it was that when we congratulated Miss Forster, she blushed and smiled and dimpled, for all the world as though she were in love with him, and had been in love with him all the time. Upon my word, I think she had. Women are strange creatures.

We were all asked to the wedding. In Brixham every one who was anybody knew everybody else who was any one. My sisters were, I truly believe, more interested in the *trousseau* than the bride herself, and I was to be best man. The coming marriage was much canvassed at afternoon tea-tables, and at our little Club over the saddler's, and the question was always asked: "Does she care for him?"

I used to ask that question myself in the early days of their engagement, but after a certain evening in August I never asked it again. I was coming home from the Club through the churchyard. Our church is on a thyme-grown hill, and the turf about it is so thick and soft that one's footsteps are noiseless.

I made no sound as I vaulted the low lichened wall, and threaded my way between the tombstones. It was at the same instant that I heard John Charrington's voice, and saw Her. May was sitting on a low flat gravestone, her face turned towards the full splendour of the western sun. Its expression ended, at once and for ever, any question of love for him; it was transfigured to a beauty I should not have believed possible, even to that beautiful little face.

John lay at her feet, and it was his voice that broke the stillness of the golden August evening.

"My dear, my dear, I believe I should come back from the dead if you wanted me!"

I coughed at once to indicate my presence, and passed on into the shadow fully enlightened.

The wedding was to be early in September. Two days before I had to run up to town on business. The train was late, of course, for we are on the South-Eastern, and as I stood grumbling with my watch in my hand, whom should I see but John Charrington and May Forster. They were walking up and down the unfrequented end of the platform, arm in arm, looking into each other's eyes, careless of the sympathetic interest of the porters.

Of course I knew better than to hesitate a moment before burying myself in the booking-office, and it was not till the train drew up at the platform, that I obtrusively passed the pair with my Gladstone, and took the corner in a first-class smoking-carriage. I did this with as good an air of not seeing them as I could assume. I pride myself on my discretion, but if John were travelling alone I wanted his company. I had it.

"Hullo, old man," came his cheery voice as he swung his bag into my carriage; "here's luck; I was expecting a dull journey!"

"Where are you off to?" I asked, discretion still bidding me turn my eyes away, though I saw, without looking, that hers were red-rimmed.

"To old Branbridge's," he answered, shutting the door and leaning out for a last word with his sweetheart.

"Oh, I wish you wouldn't go, John," she was saying in a low, earnest voice. "I feel certain something will happen."

"Do you think I should let anything happen to keep me, and the day after to-morrow our wedding-day?"

"Don't go," she answered, with a pleading intensity which would have sent my Gladstone on to the platform and me after it. But she wasn't speaking to me. John Charrington was made differently; he rarely changed his opinions, never his resolutions.

He only stroked the little ungloved hands that lay on the carriage door.

"I must, May. The old boy's been awfully good to me, and now he's dying I must go and see him, but I shall come home in time for—" the rest of the parting was lost in a whisper and in the rattling lurch of the starting train.

"You're sure to come?" she spoke as the train moved.

"Nothing shall keep me," he answered; and we steamed out. After he had seen the last of the little figure on the platform he leaned back in his corner and kept silence for a minute.

When he spoke it was to explain to me that his godfather, whose heir he was, lay dying at Peasmarsh Place, some fifty miles away, and had sent for John, and John had felt bound to go.

"I shall be surely back to-morrow," he said, "or, if not, the day after, in heaps of time. Thank Heaven, one hasn't to get up in the middle of the night to get married nowadays!"

"And suppose Mr. Branbridge dies?"

"Alive or dead I mean to be married on Thursday!" John answered, lighting a cigar and unfolding the *Times*.

At Peasmarsh station we said "good-bye," and he got out, and I saw him ride off; I went on to London, where I stayed the night.

When I got home the next afternoon, a very wet one, by the way, my sister greeted me with—

"Where's Mr. Charrington?"

"Goodness knows," I answered testily. Every man, since Cain, has resented that kind of question.

"I thought you might have heard from him," she went on, "as you're to give him away to-morrow."

"Isn't he back?" I asked, for I had confidently expected to find him at home.

"No, Geoffrey,"—my sister Fanny always had a way of jumping to conclusions, especially such conclusions as were least favourable to her fellow-creatures—"he has not returned, and, what is more, you may depend upon it he won't. You mark my words, there'll be no wedding to-morrow."

My sister Fanny has a power of annoying me which no other human being possesses.

"You mark my words," I retorted with asperity, "you had better give up making such a thundering idiot of yourself. There'll be more wedding to-morrow than ever you'll take the first part in." A prophecy which, by the way, came true.

But though I could snarl confidently to my sister, I did not feel so comfortable when, late that night, I, standing on the doorstep of John's house, heard that he had not returned. I went home gloomily through the rain. Next morning brought a brilliant blue sky, gold sun, and all such softness of air and beauty of cloud as go to make up a perfect day. I woke with a vague feeling of having gone to bed anxious, and of being rather averse to facing that anxiety in the light of full wakefulness.

But with my shaving-water came a note from John which relieved my mind and sent me up to the Forsters' with a light heart.

May was in the garden. I saw her blue gown through the hollyhocks as the lodge gates swung to behind me. So I did not go up to the house, but turned aside down the turfed path.

"He's written to you too," she said, without preliminary greeting, when I reached her side.

"Yes, I'm to meet him at the station at three, and come straight on to the church."

Her face looked pale, but there was a brightness in her eyes, and a tender quiver about the mouth that spoke of renewed happiness.

"Mr. Branbridge begged him so to stay another night that he had not the heart to refuse," she went on. "He is so kind, but I wish he hadn't stayed."

I was at the station at half-past two. I felt rather annoyed with John. It seemed a sort of slight to the beautiful girl who loved him, that he should come as it were out of breath, and with the dust of travel upon him, to take her hand, which some of us would have given the best years of our lives to take.

But when the three o'clock train glided in, and glided out again having brought no passengers to our little station, I was more than annoyed. There was no other train for thirty-five minutes; I calculated that, with much hurry, we might just get to the church in time for the ceremony; but, oh, what a fool to miss that first train! What other man could have done it?

That thirty-five minutes seemed a year, as I wandered round the station reading the advertisements and the time-tables, and the company's bye-laws, and getting more and more angry with John Charrington. This confidence in his own power of getting everything he wanted the minute he wanted it was leading him too far. I hate waiting. Every one does, but I believe I hate it more than any one else. The three thirty-five was late, of course.

I ground my pipe between my teeth and stamped with impatience as I watched the signals. Click. The signal went down. Five minutes later I flung myself into the carriage that I had brought for John.

"Drive to the church!" I said, as some one shut the door. "Mr. Charrington hasn't come by this train."

Anxiety now replaced anger. What had become of the man? Could he have been taken suddenly ill? I had never known him have a day's illness in his life. And even so he might have telegraphed. Some awful accident must have happened to him. The thought that he had played her false never—no, not for a moment—entered my head. Yes, something terrible had happened to him, and on me lay the task of telling his bride. I almost wished the carriage would upset and break my head so that some one else might tell her, not I, who—but that's nothing to do with his story.

It was five minutes to four as we drew up at the churchyard gate. A double row of eager on-lookers lined the path from lychgate to porch. I sprang from the carriage and passed up between them. Our gardener had a good front place near the door. I stopped.

"Are they waiting still, Byles?" I asked, simply to gain time, for of course I knew they were by the waiting crowd's attentive attitude.

"Waiting, sir? No, no, sir; why, it must be over by now."

"Over! Then Mr. Charrington's come?"

"To the minute, sir; must have missed you somehow, and, I say, sir," lowering his voice, "I never see Mr. John the least bit so afore, but my opinion is he's been drinking pretty free. His clothes was all dusty and his face like a sheet. I tell you I didn't like the looks of him at all, and the folks inside are saying all sorts of things. You'll see, something's gone very wrong with Mr. John, and he's tried liquor. He looked like a ghost, and in he went with his eyes straight before him, with never a look or a word for none of us; him that was always such a gentleman!"

I had never heard Byles make so long a speech. The crowd in the churchyard were talking in whispers and getting ready rice and slippers to throw at the bride and bridegroom. The ringers were ready with their hands on the ropes to ring out the merry peal as the bride and bridegroom should come out.

A murmur from the church announced them; out they came. Byles was right. John Charrington did not look himself. There was dust on his coat, his hair was disarranged. He seemed to have been in some row, for there was a black mark above his eyebrow. He was deathly pale. But his pallor was not greater than that of the bride, who might have been carved in ivory—dress, veil, orange blossoms, face and all.

As they passed out the ringers stooped—there were six of them— and then, on the ears expecting the gay wedding peal, came the slow tolling of the passing bell.

A thrill of horror at so foolish a jest from the ringers passed through us all. But the ringers themselves dropped the ropes and fled like rabbits out into the sunlight. The bride shuddered, and grey shadows came about her mouth, but the bridegroom led her on down the path where the people stood with the handfuls of rice; but the handfuls were never thrown, and the wedding-bells never rang. In vain the ringers were urged to remedy their mistake: they protested with many whispered expletives that they would see themselves further first.

In a hush like the hush in the chamber of death the bridal pair passed into their carriage and its door slammed behind them.

Then the tongues were loosed. A babel of anger, wonder, conjecture from the guests and the spectators.

"If I'd seen his condition, sir," said old Forster to me as we drove off, "I would have stretched him on the floor of the church, sir, by Heaven I would, before I'd have let him marry my daughter!"

Then he put his head out of the window.

"Drive like hell," he cried to the coachman; "don't spare the horses."

He was obeyed. We passed the bride's carriage. I forebore to look at it, and old Forster turned his head away and swore. We reached home before it.

We stood in the hall doorway, in the blazing afternoon sun, and in about half a minute we heard wheels crunching the gravel. When the carriage stopped in front of the steps old Forster and I ran down.

"Great Heaven, the carriage is empty! And yet—"

I had the door open in a minute, and this is what I saw—

No sign of John Charrington; and of May, his wife, only a huddled heap of white satin lying half on the floor of the carriage and half on the seat.

"I drove straight here, sir," said the coachman, as the bride's father lifted her out; "and I'll swear no one got out of the carriage."

We carried her into the house in her bridal dress and drew back her veil. I saw her face. Shall I ever forget it? White, white and drawn with agony and horror, bearing such a look of terror as I have never seen since except in dreams. And her hair, her radiant blonde hair, I tell you it was white like snow.

As we stood, her father and I, half mad with the horror and mystery of it, a boy came up the avenue—a telegraph boy. They brought the orange envelope to me. I tore it open.

"Mr. Charrington was thrown from the dogcart on his way to the station at half-past one. Killed on the spot!"

And he was married to May Forster in our parish church at *half-past three*, in presence of half the parish.

"I shall be married, dead or alive!"

What had passed in that carriage on the homeward drive? No one knows—no one will ever know. Oh, May! oh, my dear!

Before a week was over they laid her beside her husband in our little churchyard on the thyme-covered hill—the churchyard where they had kept their love-trysts.

Thus was accomplished John Charrington's wedding.

N o, my dear," my Uncle Abraham answered me, "no—nothing romantic ever happened to me—unless—but no: that wasn't romantic either—"

I was. To me, I being eighteen, romance was the world. My Uncle Abraham was old and lame. I followed the gaze of his faded eyes, and my own rested on a miniature that hung at his elbow-chair's right hand, a portrait of a woman, whose loveliness even the miniature-painter's art had been powerless to disguise—a woman with large lustrous eyes and perfect oval face.

I rose to look at it. I had looked at it a hundred times. Often enough in my baby days I had asked, "Who's that, uncle?" always receiving the same answer: "A lady who died long ago, my dear."

As I looked again at the picture, I asked, "Was she like this?"

"Who?"

"Your—your romance!"

Uncle Abraham looked hard at me. "Yes," he said at last. "Very—very like."

I sat down on the floor by him. "Won't you tell me about her?"

"There's nothing to tell," he said. "I think it was fancy, mostly, and folly; but it's the realest thing in my long life, my dear."

A long pause. I kept silence. "Hurry no man's cattle" is a good motto, especially with old people.

"I remember," he said in the dreamy tone always promising so well to the ear that a story delighteth—"I remember, when I was a young man, I was very lonely indeed. I never had a sweetheart. I was always lame, my dear, from quite a boy; and the girls used to laugh at me."

He sighed. Presently he went on—

"And so I got into the way of mooning off by myself in lonely places, and one of my favourite walks was up through our churchyard, which was set high on a hill in the middle of the marsh country. I liked that because I never met any one there. It's all over, years ago. I was a silly lad; but I couldn't bear of a summer evening to hear a rustle and a whisper from the other side of the hedge, or maybe a kiss as I went by.

"Well, I used to go and sit all by myself in the churchyard, which was always sweet with thyme, and quite light (on account of its being so high) long after the marshes were dark. I used to watch the bats flitting about in the red light, and wonder why God didn't make every one's legs straight and strong, and wicked follies like that. But by the time the light was gone I had always worked it off, so to speak, and could go home quietly and say my prayers without any bitterness.

"Well, one hot night in August, when I had watched the sunset fade and the crescent moon grow golden, I was just stepping over the low stone wall of the churchyard when I heard a rustle behind me. I turned round, expecting it to be a rabbit or a bird. It was a woman."

He looked at the portrait. So did I.

"Yes," he said, "that was her very face. I was a bit scared and said something—I don't know what—and she laughed and said, 'Did I think she was a ghost?' and I answered back, and I stayed talking to her over the churchyard wall till 'twas quite dark, and the glowworms were out in the wet grass all along the way home.

"Next night I saw her again; and the next night and the next. Always at twilight time; and if I passed any lovers leaning on the stiles in the marshes it was nothing to me now."

Again my uncle paused. "It's very long ago," he said slowly, "and I'm an old man; but I know what youth means, and happiness, though I was always lame, and the girls used to laugh at me. I don't know how long it went on—you don't measure time in dreams—but at last your grandfather said I looked as if I had one foot in the grave, and he would be sending me to stay with our kin at Bath and take the waters. I had to go. I could not tell my father why I would rather had died than go."

"What was her name, uncle?" I asked.

"She never would tell me her name, and why should she? I had names enough in my heart to call her by. Marriage? My dear, even then I knew marriage was not for me. But I met her night after night, always in our churchyard where the yew-trees were and the lichened gravestones. It was there we always met and always parted. The last time was the night before I went away. She was very sad, and dearer than life itself. And she said—

"'If you come back before the new moon I shall meet you here just as usual. But if the new moon shines on this grave and you are not here— you will never see me again any more.'

"She laid her hand on the yellow lichened tomb against which we had been leaning. It was an old weather-worn stone, and bore on it the inscription—

'Susannah Kingsnorth,
Ob. 1713.'

"'I shall be here.' I said.

"'I mean it,' she said, with deep and sudden seriousness, 'it is no fancy. You will be here when the new moon shines?'"

"I promised, and after a while we parted.

"I had been with my kinsfolk at Bath nearly a month. I was to go home on the next day, when, turning over a case in the parlour, I came upon that miniature. I could not speak for a minute. At last I said, with dry tongue, and heart beating to the tune of heaven and hell—

"'Who is this?'

"'That?' said my aunt. 'Oh! she was betrothed to one of our family many years ago, but she died before the wedding. They say she was a bit of a witch. A handsome one, wasn't she?'

"I looked again at the face, the lips, the eyes of my dear and lovely love, whom I was to meet to-morrow night when the new moon shone on that tomb in our churchyard.

"'Did you say she was dead?' I asked, and I hardly knew my own voice.

"'Years and years ago! Her name's on the back and her date—'

"I took the portrait from its faded red-velvet bed, and read on the back—'Susannah Kingsnorth, Ob. 1713.'

"That was in 1813." My uncle stopped short.

"What happened?" I asked breathlessly.

"I believe I had a fit," my uncle answered slowly; "at any rate, I was very ill."

"And you missed the new moon on the grave?"

"I missed the new moon on the grave."

"And you never saw her again?"

"I never saw her again—"

"But, uncle, do you really believe?—Can the dead?—was she—did you—"

My uncle took out his pipe and filled it.

"It's a long time ago," he said, "a many, many years. Old man's tales, my dear! Old man's tales! Don't you take any notice of them."

He lighted the pipe, puffed silently a moment or two, and then added: "But I know what youth means, and happiness, though I was lame, and the girls used to laugh at me."

The Mystery of the Semi-Detached

H e was waiting for her; he had been waiting an hour and a half in a dusty suburban lane, with a row of big elms on one side and some eligible building sites on the other—and far away to the south-west the twinkling yellow lights of the Crystal Palace. It was not quite like a country lane, for it had a pavement and lamp-posts, but it was not a bad place for a meeting all the same; and farther up, towards the cemetery, it was really quite rural, and almost pretty, especially in twilight. But twilight had long deepened into night, and still he waited. He loved her, and he was engaged to be married to her, with the complete disapproval of every reasonable person who had been consulted. And this half-clandestine meeting was to-night to take the place of the grudgingly sanctioned weekly interview—because a certain rich uncle was visiting at her house, and her mother was not the woman to acknowledge to a moneyed uncle, who might "go off" any day, a match so deeply ineligible as hers with him.

So he waited for her, and the chill of an unusually severe May evening entered into his bones.

The policeman passed him with but a surly response to his "Good night." The bicyclists went by him like grey ghosts with fog-horns; and it was nearly ten o'clock, and she had not come.

He shrugged his shoulders and turned towards his lodgings. His road led him by her house—desirable, commodious, semi-detached—and he walked slowly as he neared it. She might, even now, be coming out. But she was not. There was no sign of movement about the house, no sign of life, no lights even in the windows. And her people were not early people.

He paused by the gate, wondering.

Then he noticed that the front door was open—wide open—and the street lamp shone a little way into the dark hall. There was something about all this that did not please him—that scared him a little, indeed. The house had a gloomy and deserted air. It was obviously impossible that it harboured a rich uncle. The old man must have left early. In which case—

He walked up the path of patent-glazed tiles, and listened. No sign of life. He passed into the hall. There was no light anywhere. Where was everybody, and why was the front door open? There was no one in the drawing-room, the dining-room and the study (nine feet by seven) were equally blank. Every one was out, evidently. But the unpleasant sense that he was, perhaps, not the first casual visitor to walk through that open door impelled him to look through the house before he went away and closed it after him. So he went upstairs, and at the door of the first bedroom he came to he struck a wax match, as he had done in the sitting-rooms. Even as he did so he felt that he was not alone. And he was prepared to see *something*; but for what he saw he was not prepared. For what he saw lay on the bed, in a white loose gown—and it was his sweetheart, and its throat was cut from ear to ear. He doesn't know what happened then, nor how he got downstairs and into the street; but he got out somehow, and the policeman found him in a fit, under the lamp-post at the corner of the street. He couldn't speak when they picked him up, and he passed the night in the police-cells, because the policeman had seen plenty of drunken men before, but never one in a fit.

The next morning he was better, though still very white and shaky. But the tale he told the magistrate was convincing, and they sent a couple of constables with him to her house.

There was no crowd about it as he had fancied there would be, and the blinds were not down.

As he stood, dazed, in front of the door, it opened, and she came out.

He held on to the door-post for support.

"*She's* all right, you see," said the constable, who had found him under the lamp. "I told you you was drunk, but you *would* know best—"

When he was alone with her he told her—not all—for that would not bear telling—but how he had come into the commodious semi-detached, and how he had found the door open and the lights out, and that he had been into that long back room facing the stairs, and had seen something—in even trying to hint at which he turned sick and broke down and had to have brandy given him.

"But, my dearest," she said, "I dare say the house was dark, for we were all at the Crystal Palace with my uncle, and no doubt the door was open, for the maids *will* run out if they're left. But you could not have been in that room, because I locked it when I came away, and the key was in my pocket. I dressed in a hurry and I left all my odds and ends lying about."

"I know," he said; "I saw a green scarf on a chair, and some long brown gloves, and a lot of hairpins and ribbons, and a prayer-book, and a lace handkerchief on the dressing-table. Why, I even noticed the almanack on the mantelpiece—October 21. At least it couldn't be that, because this is May. And yet it was. Your almanac is at October 21, isn't it?"

"No, of course it isn't," she said, smiling rather anxiously; "but all the other things were just as you say. You must have had a dream, or a vision, or something."

He was a very ordinary, commonplace, City young man, and he didn't believe in visions, but he never rested day or night till he got his sweetheart and her mother away from that commodious semi-detached, and settled them in a quite distant suburb. In the course of the removal he incidentally married her, and the mother went on living with them.

His nerves must have been a good bit shaken, because he was very queer for a long time, and was always inquiring if any one had taken the desirable semi-detached; and when an old stockbroker with a family took it, he went the length of calling on the old gentleman and imploring him by all that he held dear, not to live in that fatal house.

"Why?" said the stockbroker, not unnaturally.

And then he got so vague and confused, between trying to tell why and trying not to tell why, that the stockbroker showed him out, and thanked his God he was not such a fool as to allow a lunatic to stand in the way of his taking that really remarkably cheap and desirable semi-detached residence.

Now the curious and quite inexplicable part of this story is that when she came down to breakfast on the morning of the 22nd of October she found him looking like death, with the morning paper in his hand. He caught hers—he couldn't speak, and pointed to the paper. And there she read that on the night of the 21st a young lady, the stockbroker's daughter, had been found, with her throat cut from ear to ear, on the bed in the long back bedroom facing the stairs of that desirable semi-detached.

From the Dead

"But true or not true, your brother is a scoundrel. No man—no decent man—tells such things."

"He did not tell me. How dare you suppose it? I found the letter in his desk; and she being my friend and you being her lover, I never thought there could be any harm in my reading her letter to my brother. Give me back the letter. I was a fool to tell you."

Ida Helmont held out her hand for the letter.

"Not yet," I said, and I went to the window. The dull red of a London sunset burned on the paper, as I read in the quaint, dainty handwriting I knew so well and had kissed so often—

> Dear,
>
> I do—I do love you; but it's impossible. I must marry Arthur. My honour is engaged. If he would only set me free—but he never will. He loves me so foolishly. But as for me, it is you I love—body, soul, and spirit. There is no one in my heart but you. I think of you all day, and dream of you all night. And we must part. And that is the way of the world. Good-bye!
>
> Yours, yours, yours,
> Elvire

I had seen the handwriting, indeed, often enough. But the passion written there was new to me. That I had not seen.

I turned from the window wearily. My sitting-room looked strange to me. There were my books, my reading-lamp, my untasted dinner still on the table, as I had left it when I rose to dissemble my surprise at Ida Helmont's visit—Ida Helmont, who now sat in my easy-chair looking at me quietly.

"Well—do you give me no thanks?"

"You put a knife in my heart, and then ask for thanks?"

"Pardon me," she said, throwing up her chin. "I have done nothing but show you the truth. For that one should expect no gratitude—may I ask, out of mere curiosity, what you intend to do?"

"Your brother will tell you—"

She rose suddenly, pale to the lips.

"You will not tell my brother?" she began.

"That you have read his private letters? Certainly not!"

She came towards me—her gold hair flaming in the sunset light.

"Why are you so angry with me?" she said. "Be reasonable. What else could I do?"

"I don't know."

"Would it have been right not to tell you?"

"I don't know. I only know that you've put the sun out, and I haven't got used to the dark yet."

"Believe me," she said, coming still nearer to me, and laying her hands in the lightest light touch on my shoulders, "believe me, she never loved you."

There was a softness in her tone that irritated and stimulated me. I moved gently back, and her hands fell by her sides.

"I beg your pardon," I said. "I have behaved very badly. You were quite right to come, and I am not ungrateful. Will you post a letter for me?"

I sat down and wrote—

"I give you back your freedom. The only gift of mine that can please you now.

ARTHUR

I held the sheet out to Miss Helmont, and, when she had glanced at it, I sealed, stamped, and addressed it.

"Good-bye," I said then, and gave her the letter. As the door closed behind her I sank into my chair, and I am not ashamed to say that I cried like a child or a fool over my lost plaything—the little dark-haired woman who loved some one else with "body, soul, and spirit."

I did not hear the door open or any foot on the floor, and therefore I started when a voice behind me said—

"Are you so very unhappy? Oh, Arthur, don't think I am not sorry for you!"

"I don't want any one to be sorry for me, Miss Helmont," I said.

She was silent a moment. Then, with a quick, sudden, gentle movement she leaned down and kissed my forehead—and I heard the door softly close. Then I knew that the beautiful Miss Helmont loved me.

At first that thought only fleeted by—a light cloud against a grey sky—but the next day reason woke, and said—

"Was Miss Helmont speaking the truth? Was it possible that—?"

I determined to see Elvire, to know from her own lips whether by happy fortune this blow came, not from her, but from a woman in whom love might have killed honesty.

I walked from Hampstead to Gower Street. As I trod its long length, I saw a figure in pink come out of one of the houses. It was Elvire. She walked in front of me to the corner of Store Street. There she met Oscar Helmont. They turned and met me face to face, and I saw all I needed to see. They loved each other. Ida Helmont had spoken the truth. I bowed and passed on. Before six months were gone they were married, and before a year was over I had married Ida Helmont.

What did it I don't know. Whether it was remorse for having, even for half a day, dreamed that she could be so base as to forge a lie to gain a lover, or whether it was her beauty, or the sweet flattery of the preference of a woman who had half her acquaintances at her feet, I don't know; anyhow, my thoughts turned to her as to their natural home. My heart, too, took that road, and before very long I loved her as I had never loved Elvire. Let no one doubt that I loved her—as I shall never love again, please God!

There never was any one like her. She was brave and beautiful, witty and wise, and beyond all measure adorable. She was the only woman in the world. There was a frankness—a largeness of heart—about her that made all other women seem small and contemptible. She loved me and I worshipped her. I married her, I stayed with her for three golden weeks, and then I left her. Why?

Because she told me the truth. It was one night—late—we had sat all the evening in the verandah of our seaside lodging watching the moonlight on the water and listening to the soft sound of the sea on the sand. I have never been so happy; I never shall be happy any more, I hope.

"Heart's heart," she said, leaning her gold head against my shoulder, "how much do you love me?"

"How much?"

"Yes—how much? I want to know what place it is I hold in your heart. Am I more to you than any one else?"

"My love!"

"More than yourself?"

"More than my life!"

"I believe you," she said. Then she drew a long breath, and took my hands in hers. "It can make no difference. Nothing in heaven or earth can come between us now."

"Nothing," I said. "But, sweet, my wife, what is it?"

For she was deathly pale.

"I must tell you," she said; "I cannot hide anything now from you, because I am yours—body, soul, and spirit."

The phrase was an echo that stung me.

The moonlight shone on her gold hair, her warm, soft, gold hair, and on her pale face.

"Arthur," she said, "you remember my coming to you at Hampstead with that letter?"

"Yes, my sweet, and I remember how you—"

"Arthur!"—she spoke fast and low—"Arthur, that letter was a forgery. She never wrote it. I—"

She stopped, for I had risen and flung her hands from me, and stood looking at her. God help me! I thought it was anger at the lie I felt. I know now it was only wounded vanity that smarted in me. That *I* should have been tricked, that *I* should have been deceived, that *I* should have been led on to make a fool of myself! That *I* should have married the woman who had befooled me! At that moment she was no longer the wife I adored—she was only a woman who had forged a letter and tricked me into marrying her.

I spoke; I denounced her; I said I would never speak to her again. I felt it was rather creditable in me to be so angry. I said I would have no more to do with a liar and forger.

I don't know whether I expected her to creep to my knees and implore forgiveness. I think I had some vague idea that I could by-and-by consent with dignity to forgive and forget. I did not mean what I said. No, no; I did not mean a word of it. While I was saying it I was longing for her to weep and fall at my feet, that I might raise her and hold her in my arms again.

But she did not fall at my feet; she stood quietly looking at me.

"Arthur," she said, as I paused for breath, "let me explain—she—I—"

"There is nothing to explain," I said hotly, still with that foolish sense of there being something rather noble in my indignation, as one feels when one calls one's self a miserable sinner. "You are a liar and forger, and that is enough for me. I will never speak to you again. You have wrecked my life—"

"Do you mean that?" she said, interrupting me, and leaning forward to look at me. Tears lay on her cheeks, but she was not crying now.

I hesitated. I longed to take her in my arms and say—"Lay your head here, my darling, and cry here, and know how I love you."

But instead I kept silence.

"*Do* you mean it?" she persisted.

Then she put her hand on my arm. I longed to clasp it and draw her to me.

Instead, I shook it off, and said—

"Mean it? Yes—of course I mean it. Don't touch me, please! You have ruined my life."

She turned away without a word, went into our room, and shut the door.

I longed to follow her, to tell her that if there was anything to forgive I forgave it.

Instead, I went out on the beach, and walked away under the cliffs.

The moonlight and the solitude, however, presently brought me to a better mind. Whatever she had done had been done for love of me—I knew that. I would go home and tell her so—tell her that whatever she had done she was my dearest life, my heart's one treasure. True, my ideal of her was shattered, but, even as she was, what was the whole world of women compared to her? I hurried back, but in my resentment and evil temper I had walked far, and the way back was very long. I had been parted from her for three hours by the time I opened the door of the little house where we lodged. The house was dark and very still. I slipped off my shoes and crept up the narrow stairs, and opened the door of our room quite softly. Perhaps she would have cried herself to sleep, and I would lean over her and waken her with my kisses and beg her to forgive me. Yes, it had come to that now.

I went into the room—I went towards the bed. She was not there. She was not in the room, as one glance showed me. She was not in the house, as I knew in two minutes. When I had wasted a priceless hour in searching the town for her, I found a note on the dressing-table—

"Good-bye! Make the best of what is left of your life. I will spoil it no more."

She was gone, utterly gone. I rushed to town by the earliest morning train, only to find that her people knew nothing of her. Advertisement failed. Only a tramp said he had met a white lady on the cliff, and a fisherman brought me a handkerchief marked with her name that he had found on the beach.

I searched the country far and wide, but I had to go back to London at last, and the months went by. I won't say much about those months, because even the memory of that suffering turns me faint and sick at heart. The police and detectives and the Press failed me utterly. Her friends could not help me, and were, moreover, wildly indignant with me, especially her brother, now living very happily with my first love.

I don't know how I got through those long weeks and months. I tried to write; I tried to read; I tried to live the life of a reasonable human being. But it was impossible. I could not endure the companionship of my kind. Day and night I almost saw her face—almost heard her voice. I took long walks in the country, and her figure was always just round the next turn of the road—in the next glade of the wood. But I never quite saw her—never quite heard her. I believe I was not altogether sane at that time. At last, one morning as I was setting out for one of those long walks that had no goal but weariness, I met a telegraph boy, and took the red envelope from his hand.

On the pink paper inside was written—

Come to me at once. I am dying. You must come.

IDA.
Apinshaw
Farm, Mellor, Derbyshire

There was a train at twelve to Marple, the nearest station. I took it. I tell you there are some things that cannot be written about. My life for those long months was one of them, that journey was another. What had her life been for those months? That question troubled me, as one is troubled in every nerve at the sight of a surgical operation or a wound inflicted on a being dear to one. But the overmastering sensation was joy—intense, unspeakable joy. She was alive! I should see her again. I took out the telegram and looked at it: "I am dying." I simply did not believe it. She could not die till she had seen me. And if she had lived all those months without me, she could live now, when I was with her again, when she knew of the hell I had endured apart from her, and the heaven of our meeting. She must live. I would not let her die.

There was a long drive over bleak hills. Dark, jolting, infinitely wearisome. At last we stopped before a long, low building, where one or two lights gleamed faintly. I sprang out.

The door opened. A blaze of light made me blink and draw back. A woman was standing in the doorway.

"Art thee Arthur Marsh?" she said.

"Yes."

"Then, th'art ower late. She's dead."

II

I WENT INTO THE HOUSE, walked to the fire, and held out my hands to it mechanically, for, though the night was May, I was cold to the bone. There were some folks standing round the fire and lights flickering. Then an old woman came forward with the northern instinct of hospitality.

"Thou'rt tired," she said, "and mazed-like. Have a sup o' tea."

I burst out laughing. It was too funny. I had travelled two hundred miles to see *her*; and she was dead, and they offered me tea. They drew back from me as if I had been a wild beast, but I could not stop laughing. Then a hand was laid on my shoulder, and some one led me into a dark room, lighted a lamp, set me in a chair, and sat down opposite me. It was a bare parlour, coldly furnished with rush chairs and much-polished tables and presses. I caught my breath, and grew suddenly grave, and looked at the woman who sat opposite me.

"I was Miss Ida's nurse," said she; "and she told me to send for you. Who are you?"

"Her husband—"

The woman looked at me with hard eyes, where intense surprise struggled with resentment. "Then, may God forgive you!" she said. "What you've done I don't know; but it'll be 'ard work forgivin' *you*— even for *Him*!"

"Tell me," I said, "my wife—"

"Tell you?" The bitter contempt in the woman's tone did not hurt me; what was it to the self-contempt that had gnawed my heart all these months? "Tell you? Yes, I'll tell you. Your wife was that ashamed of you, she never so much as told me she was married. She let me think anything I pleased sooner than that. She just come 'ere an' she said, 'Nurse, take care of me, for I am in mortal trouble. And don't let them know where I am,' says she. An' me bein' well married to an honest man, and well-to-do here, I was able to do it, by the blessing."

"Why didn't you send for me before?" It was a cry of anguish wrung from me.

"I'd *never* 'a sent for you—it was *her* doin'. Oh, to think as God A'mighty's made men able to measure out such-like pecks o' trouble for us womenfolk! Young man, I dunno what you did to 'er to make 'er leave you; but it muster bin something cruel, for she loved the ground you walked on. She useter sit day after day, a-lookin' at your picture an' talkin' to it an' kissin' of it, when she thought I wasn't takin' no notice, and cryin' till she made me cry too. She useter cry all night 'most. An' one day, when I tells 'er to pray to God to 'elp 'er through 'er trouble, she outs with *your* putty face on a card, she doez, an', says she, with her poor little smile, 'That's my god, Nursey,' she says."

"Don't!" I said feebly, putting out my hands to keep off the torture; "not any more, not now."

"*Don't?*" she repeated. She had risen and was walking up and down the room with clasped hands—"don't, indeed! No, I won't; but I shan't forget you! I tell you I've had you in my prayers time and again, when I thought you'd made a light-o'-love o' my darling. I shan't drop you outer them now I know she was your own wedded wife as you chucked away when you'd tired of her, and left 'er to eat 'er 'art out with longin' for you. Oh! I pray to God above us to pay you scot and lot for all you done to 'er! You killed my pretty. The price will be required of you, young man, even to the uttermost farthing! O God in heaven, make him suffer! Make him feel it!"

She stamped her foot as she passed me. I stood quite still; I bit my lip till I tasted the blood hot and salt on my tongue.

"She was nothing to you!" cried the woman, walking faster up and down between the rush chairs and the table; "any fool can see that with half an eye. You didn't love her, so you don't feel nothin' now; but some day you'll care for some one, and then you shall know what she felt—if there's any justice in heaven!"

I, too, rose, walked across the room, and leaned against the wall. I heard her words without understanding them.

"Can't you feel *nothin'*? Are you mader stone? Come an' look at 'er lyin' there so quiet. She don't fret arter the likes o' you no more now. She won't sit no more a-lookin' outer winder an' sayin' nothin'—only droppin' 'er tears one by one, slow, slow on her lap. Come an' see 'er;

come an' see what you done to my pretty—an' then ye can go. Nobody wants you 'ere. *She* don't want you now. But p'r'aps you'd like to see 'er safe underground fust? I'll be bound you'll put a big slab on 'er—to make sure *she* don't rise again."

I turned on her. Her thin face was white with grief and impotent rage. Her claw-like hands were clenched.

"Woman," I said, "have mercy!"

She paused, and looked at me.

"Eh?" she said.

"Have mercy!" I said again.

"Mercy? You should 'a thought o' that before. You 'adn't no mercy on 'er. She loved you—she died lovin' you. An' if I wasn't a Christian woman, I'd kill you for it—like the rat you are! That I would, though I 'ad to swing for it arterwards."

I caught the woman's hands and held them fast, in spite of her resistance.

"Don't you understand?" I said savagely. "We loved each other. She died loving me. I have to live loving her. And it's *her* you pity. I tell you it was all a mistake—a stupid, stupid mistake. Take me to her, and for pity's sake let me be left alone with her."

She hesitated; then said in a voice only a shade less hard—

"Well, come along, then."

We moved towards the door. As she opened it a faint, weak cry fell on my ear. My heart stood still.

"What's that?" I asked, stopping on the threshold.

"Your child," she said shortly.

That, too! Oh, my love! oh, my poor love! All these long months!

"She allus said she'd send for you when she'd got over her trouble," the woman said as we climbed the stairs. "'I'd like him to see his little baby, nurse,' she says; 'our little baby. It'll be all right when the baby's born,' she says. 'I know he'll come to me then. You'll see.' And I never said nothin'—not thinkin' you'd come if she was your leavins, and not dreamin' as you could be 'er husband an' could stay away from 'er a hour—her bein' as she was. Hush!"

She drew a key from her pocket and fitted it to the lock. She opened the door and I followed her in. It was a large, dark room, full of old-fashioned furniture. There were wax candles in brass candlesticks and a smell of lavender.

The big four-post bed was covered with white.

"My lamb—my poor pretty lamb!" said the woman, beginning to cry for the first time as she drew back the sheet. "Don't she look beautiful?"

I stood by the bedside. I looked down on my wife's face. Just so I had seen it lie on the pillow beside me in the early morning when the wind and the dawn came up from beyond the sea. She did not look like one dead. Her lips were still red, and it seemed to me that a tinge of colour lay on her cheek. It seemed to me, too, that if I kissed her she would wake, and put her slight hand on my neck, and lay her cheek against mine—and that we should tell each other everything, and weep together, and understand and be comforted.

So I stooped and laid my lips to hers as the old nurse stole from the room.

But the red lips were like marble, and she did not wake. She will not wake now ever any more.

I tell you again there are some things that cannot be written.

III

I LAY THAT NIGHT IN a big room filled with heavy, dark furniture, in a great four-poster hung with heavy, dark curtains—a bed the counterpart of that other bed from whose side they had dragged me at last.

They fed me, I believe, and the old nurse was kind to me. I think she saw now that it is not the dead who are to be pitied most.

I lay at last in the big, roomy bed, and heard the household noises grow fewer and die out, the little wail of my child sounding latest. They had brought the child to me, and I had held it in my arms, and bowed my head over its tiny face and frail fingers. I did not love it then. I told myself it had cost me her life. But my heart told me that it was I who had done that. The tall clock at the stairhead sounded the hours—eleven, twelve, one, and still I could not sleep. The room was dark and very still.

I had not been able to look at my life quietly. I had been full of the intoxication of grief—a real drunkenness, more merciful than the calm that comes after.

Now I lay still as the dead woman in the next room, and looked at what was left of my life. I lay still, and thought, and thought, and thought. And in those hours I tasted the bitterness of death. It must have been about two that I first became aware of a slight sound that was not the ticking of the clock. I say I first became aware, and yet I knew perfectly that I had heard that sound more than once before, and had yet determined not to hear it, *because it came from the next room*—the room where the corpse lay.

And I did not wish to hear that sound, because I knew it meant that I was nervous—miserably nervous—a coward and a brute. It meant that I, having killed my wife as surely as though I had put a knife in her breast, had now sunk so low as to be afraid of her dead body—the dead body that lay in the room next to mine. The heads of the beds were placed against the same wall; and from that wall I had fancied I heard slight, slight, almost inaudible sounds. So when I say that I became aware of them I mean that I at last heard a sound so distinct as to leave no room for doubt or question. It brought me to a sitting position in the bed, and the drops of sweat gathered heavily on my forehead and fell on my cold hands as I held my breath and listened.

I don't know how long I sat there—there was no further sound—and at last my tense muscles relaxed, and I fell back on the pillow.

"You fool!" I said to myself; "dead or alive, is she not your darling, your heart's heart? Would you not go near to die of joy if she came to you? Pray God to let her spirit come back and tell you she forgives you!"

"I wish she would come," myself answered in words, while every fibre of my body and mind shrank and quivered in denial.

I struck a match, lighted a candle, and breathed more freely as I looked at the polished furniture—the commonplace details of an ordinary room. Then I thought of her, lying alone, so near me, so quiet under the white sheet. She was dead; she would not wake or move. But suppose she did move? Suppose she turned back the sheet and got up, and walked across the floor and turned the door-handle?

As I thought it, I heard—plainly, unmistakably heard—the door of the chamber of death open slowly—I heard slow steps in the passage, slow, heavy steps—I heard the touch of hands on my door outside, uncertain hands, that felt for the latch.

Sick with terror, I lay clenching the sheet in my hands.

I knew well enough what would come in when that door opened—that door on which my eyes were fixed. I dreaded to look, yet I dared not turn away my eyes. The door opened slowly, slowly, slowly, and the figure of my dead wife came in. It came straight towards the bed, and stood at the bed-foot in its white grave-clothes, with the white bandage under its chin. There was a scent of lavender. Its eyes were wide open and looked at me with love unspeakable.

I could have shrieked aloud.

My wife spoke. It was the same dear voice that I had loved so to hear, but it was very weak and faint now; and now I trembled as I listened.

"You aren't afraid of me, darling, are you, though I am dead? I heard all you said to me when you came, but I couldn't answer. But now I've come back from the dead to tell you. I wasn't really so bad as you thought me. Elvire had told me she loved Oscar. I only wrote the letter to make it easier for you. I was too proud to tell you when you were so angry, but I am not proud any more now. You'll love me again now, won't you, now I'm dead? One always forgives dead people."

The poor ghost's voice was hollow and faint. Abject terror paralyzed me. I could answer nothing.

"Say you forgive me," the thin, monotonous voice went on; "say you love me again."

I had to speak. Coward as I was, I did manage to stammer—

"Yes; I love you. I have always loved you, God help me!"

The sound of my own voice reassured me, and I ended more firmly than I began. The figure by the bed swayed a little unsteadily.

"I suppose," she said wearily, "you would be afraid, now I am dead, if I came round to you and kissed you?"

She made a movement as though she would have come to me.

Then I did shriek aloud, again and again, and covered my face with the sheet, and wound it round my head and body, and held it with all my force.

There was a moment's silence. Then I heard my door close, and then a sound of feet and of voices, and I heard something heavy fall. I disentangled my head from the sheet. My room was empty. Then reason came back to me. I leaped from the bed.

"Ida, my darling, come back! I am not afraid! I love you! Come back! Come back!"

I sprang to my door and flung it open. Some one was bringing a light along the passage. On the floor, outside the door of the death-chamber, was a huddled heap—the corpse, in its grave-clothes. Dead, dead, dead.

SHE IS BURIED IN MELLOR churchyard, and there is no stone over her.

Now, whether it was catalepsy—as the doctors said—or whether my love came back even from the dead to me who loved her, I shall never know; but this I know—that, if I had held out my arms to her as she stood at my bed-foot—if I had said, "Yes, even from the grave, my darling—from hell itself, come back, come back to me!"—if I had had room in my coward's heart for anything but the unreasoning terror that killed love in that hour, I should not now be here alone. I shrank from her—I feared her—I would not take her to my heart. And now she will not come to me any more.

Why do I go on living?

You see, there is the child. It is four years old now, and it has never spoken and never smiled.

Man-Size in Marble

Although every word of this story is as true as despair, I do not expect people to believe it. Nowadays a "rational explanation" is required before belief is possible. Let me then, at once, offer the "rational explanation" which finds most favour among those who have heard the tale of my life's tragedy. It is held that we were "under a delusion," Laura and I, on that 31st of October; and that this supposition places the whole matter on a satisfactory and believable basis. The reader can judge, when he, too, has heard my story, how far this is an "explanation," and in what sense it is "rational." There were three who took part in this: Laura and I and another man. The other man still lives, and can speak to the truth of the least credible part of my story.

I never in my life knew what it was to have as much money as I required to supply the most ordinary needs—good colours, books, and cab-fares—and when we were married we knew quite well that we should only be able to live at all by "strict punctuality and attention to business." I used to paint in those days, and Laura used to write, and we felt sure we could keep the pot at least simmering. Living in town was out of the question, so we went to look for a cottage in the country, which should be at once sanitary and picturesque. So rarely do these two qualities meet in one cottage that our search was for some time quite fruitless. We tried advertisements, but most of the desirable rural residences which we did look at proved to be lacking in both essentials, and when a cottage chanced to have drains it always had stucco as well and was shaped like a tea-caddy. And if we found a vine or rose-covered porch, corruption invariably lurked within. Our minds got so befogged by the eloquence of house-agents and the rival disadvantages of the fever-traps and outrages to beauty which we had seen and scorned, that I very much doubt whether either of us, on our wedding morning, knew the difference between a house and a haystack. But when we got away from friends and house-agents, on our honeymoon, our wits grew clear again, and we knew a pretty cottage when at last we saw one. It was at Brenzett—a little village set on a hill over against the southern marshes. We had gone there, from the seaside village where we were staying, to see the church, and two fields from the church we found this cottage. It stood quite by itself, about two miles from the village. It was a long, low building, with rooms sticking out in unexpected places. There was a bit of stone-work—ivy-covered and moss-grown, just two old rooms, all that was left of a big house that had once stood there—and round this stone-work the house had grown up. Stripped of its roses and jasmine it would have been hideous. As it stood it was charming, and after a brief examination we took it. It was absurdly cheap. The rest of our honeymoon we spent in grubbing about in second-hand shops in the county town, picking up bits of old oak and Chippendale chairs for our furnishing. We wound up with a run up to town and a visit to Liberty's, and soon the low oak-beamed lattice-windowed rooms began to be home. There was a jolly old-fashioned garden, with grass paths, and no end of hollyhocks and sunflowers, and big lilies. From the window you could see the marsh-pastures, and beyond them the blue, thin line of the sea. We were as happy as the summer was glorious, and settled down into work sooner than we ourselves expected. I was never tired of sketching the view and the wonderful cloud effects from the open lattice, and Laura would sit at the table and write verses about them, in which I mostly played the part of foreground.

We got a tall old peasant woman to do for us. Her face and figure were good, though her cooking was of the homeliest; but she understood all about gardening, and told us all the old names of the coppices and cornfields, and the stories of the smugglers and highwaymen, and, better still, of the "things that walked," and of the "sights" which met one in lonely glens of a starlight night. She was a great comfort to us, because Laura hated housekeeping as much as I loved folklore, and we soon came to leave all the domestic business to Mrs. Dorman, and to use her legends in little magazine stories which brought in the jingling guinea.

We had three months of married happiness, and did not have a single quarrel. One October evening I had been down to smoke a pipe with the doctor—our only neighbour—a pleasant young Irishman. Laura had stayed at home to finish a comic sketch of a village episode for the *Monthly Marplot*. I left her laughing over her own jokes, and came in to find her a crumpled heap of pale muslin weeping on the window seat.

"Good heavens, my darling, what's the matter?" I cried, taking her in my arms. She leaned her little dark head against my shoulder and went on crying. I had never seen her cry before—we had always been so happy, you see—and I felt sure some frightful misfortune had happened.

"What *is* the matter? Do speak."

"It's Mrs. Dorman," she sobbed.

"What has she done?" I inquired, immensely relieved.

"She says she must go before the end of the month, and she says her niece is ill; she's gone down to see her now, but I don't believe that's the reason, because her niece is always ill. I believe some one has been setting her against us. Her manner was so queer—"

"Never mind, Pussy," I said; "whatever you do, don't cry, or I shall have to cry too, to keep you in countenance, and then you'll never respect your man again!"

She dried her eyes obediently on my handkerchief, and even smiled faintly.

"But you see," she went on, "it is really serious, because these village people are so sheepy, and if one won't do a thing you may be quite sure none of the others will. And I shall have to cook the dinners, and wash up the hateful greasy plates; and you'll have to carry cans of water about, and clean the boots and knives—and we shall never have any time for work, or earn any money, or anything. We shall have to work all day, and only be able to rest when we are waiting for the kettle to boil!"

I represented to her that even if we had to perform these duties, the day would still present some margin for other toils and recreations. But she refused to see the matter in any but the greyest light. She was very unreasonable, my Laura, but I could not have loved her any more if she had been as reasonable as Whately.

"I'll speak to Mrs. Dorman when she comes back, and see if I can't come to terms with her," I said. "Perhaps she wants a rise in her screw. It will be all right. Let's walk up to the church."

The church was a large and lonely one, and we loved to go there, especially upon bright nights. The path skirted a wood, cut through it once, and ran along the crest of the hill through two meadows, and round the churchyard wall, over which the old yews loomed in black masses of shadow. This path, which was partly paved, was called "the bier-balk," for it had long been the way by which the corpses had been carried to burial. The churchyard was richly treed, and was shaded by great elms which stood just outside and stretched their majestic arms in benediction over the happy dead. A large, low porch let one into the building by a Norman doorway and a heavy oak door studded with iron. Inside, the arches rose into darkness, and between them the reticulated windows, which stood out white in the moonlight. In the chancel, the windows were of rich glass, which showed in faint light their noble colouring, and made the black oak of the choir pews hardly more solid than the shadows. But on each side of the altar lay a grey marble figure of a knight in full plate armour lying upon a low slab, with hands held up in everlasting prayer, and these figures, oddly enough, were always to be seen if there was any glimmer of light in the church. Their names were lost, but the peasants told of them that they had been fierce and wicked men, marauders by land and sea, who had been the scourge of their time, and had been guilty of deeds so foul that the house they had lived in—the big house, by the way, that had stood on the site of our cottage—had been stricken by lightning and the vengeance of Heaven. But for all that, the gold of their heirs had bought them a place in the church. Looking at the bad hard faces reproduced in the marble, this story was easily believed.

The church looked at its best and weirdest on that night, for the shadows of the yew trees fell through the windows upon the floor of the nave and touched the pillars with tattered shade. We sat down together without speaking, and watched the solemn beauty of the old church, with some of that awe which inspired its early builders. We walked to the chancel and looked at the sleeping warriors. Then we rested some time on the stone seat in the porch, looking out over the stretch of quiet moonlit meadows, feeling in every fibre of our being the peace of the night and of our happy love; and came away at last with a sense that even scrubbing and blackleading were but small troubles at their worst.

Mrs. Dorman had come back from the village, and I at once invited her to a *tête-à-tête*.

"Now, Mrs. Dorman," I said, when I had got her into my painting room, "what's all this about your not staying with us?"

"I should be glad to get away, sir, before the end of the month," she answered, with her usual placid dignity.

"Have you any fault to find, Mrs. Dorman?"

"None at all, sir; you and your lady have always been most kind, I'm sure—"

"Well, what is it? Are your wages not high enough?"

"No, sir, I gets quite enough."

"Then why not stay?"

"I'd rather not"—with some hesitation—"my niece is ill."

"But your niece has been ill ever since we came."

No answer. There was a long and awkward silence. I broke it.

"Can't you stay for another month?" I asked.

"No, sir. I'm bound to go by Thursday."

And this was Monday!

"Well, I must say, I think you might have let us know before. There's no time now to get any one else, and your mistress is not fit to do heavy housework. Can't you stay till next week?"

"I might be able to come back next week."

I was now convinced that all she wanted was a brief holiday, which we should have been willing enough to let her have, as soon as we could get a substitute.

"But why must you go this week?" I persisted. "Come, out with it."

Mrs. Dorman drew the little shawl, which she always wore, tightly across her bosom, as though she were cold. Then she said, with a sort of effort—

"They say, sir, as this was a big house in Catholic times, and there was a many deeds done here."

The nature of the "deeds" might be vaguely inferred from the inflection of Mrs. Dorman's voice—which was enough to make one's blood run cold. I was glad that Laura was not in the room. She was always nervous, as highly-strung natures are, and I felt that these tales about our house, told by this old peasant woman, with her impressive manner and contagious credulity, might have made our home less dear to my wife.

"Tell me all about it, Mrs. Dorman," I said; "you needn't mind about telling me. I'm not like the young people who make fun of such things."

Which was partly true.

"Well, sir"—she sank her voice—"you may have seen in the church, beside the altar, two shapes."

"You mean the effigies of the knights in armour," I said cheerfully.

"I mean them two bodies, drawed out man-size in marble," she returned, and I had to admit that her description was a thousand times more graphic than mine, to say nothing of a certain weird force and uncanniness about the phrase "drawed out man-size in marble."

"They do say, as on All Saints' Eve them two bodies sits up on their slabs, and gets off of them, and then walks down the aisle, *in their marble*"—(another good phrase, Mrs. Dorman)—"and as the church clock strikes eleven they walks out of the church door, and over the graves, and along the bier-balk, and if it's a wet night there's the marks of their feet in the morning."

"And where do they go?" I asked, rather fascinated.

"They comes back here to their home, sir, and if any one meets them—"

"Well, what then?" I asked.

But no—not another word could I get from her, save that her niece was ill and she must go. After what I had heard I scorned to discuss the niece, and tried to get from Mrs. Dorman more details of the legend. I could get nothing but warnings.

"Whatever you do, sir, lock the door early on All Saints' Eve, and make the cross-sign over the doorstep and on the windows."

"But has any one ever seen these things?" I persisted.

"That's not for me to say. I know what I know, sir."

"Well, who was here last year?"

"No one, sir; the lady as owned the house only stayed here in summer, and she always went to London a full month afore *the* night. And I'm sorry to inconvenience you and your lady, but my niece is ill and I must go on Thursday."

I could have shaken her for her absurd reiteration of that obvious fiction, after she had told me her real reasons.

She was determined to go, nor could our united entreaties move her in the least.

I did not tell Laura the legend of the shapes that "walked in their marble," partly because a legend concerning our house might perhaps trouble my wife, and partly, I think, from some more occult reason. This was not quite the same to me as any other story, and I did not want to talk about it till the day was over. I had very soon ceased to think of the legend, however. I was painting a portrait of Laura, against the lattice window, and I could not think of much else. I had got a splendid background of yellow and grey sunset, and was working away with enthusiasm at her face. On Thursday Mrs. Dorman went. She relented, at parting, so far as to say—

"Don't you put yourself about too much, ma'am, and if there's any little thing I can do next week, I'm sure I shan't mind."

From which I inferred that she wished to come back to us after Halloween. Up to the last she adhered to the fiction of the niece with touching fidelity.

Thursday passed off pretty well. Laura showed marked ability in the matter of steak and potatoes, and I confess that my knives, and the plates, which I insisted upon washing, were better done than I had dared to expect.

Friday came. It is about what happened on that Friday that this is written. I wonder if I should have believed it, if any one had told it to me. I will write the story of it as quickly and plainly as I can. Everything that happened on that day is burnt into my brain. I shall not forget anything, nor leave anything out.

I got up early, I remember, and lighted the kitchen fire, and had just achieved a smoky success, when my little wife came running down, as sunny and sweet as the clear October morning itself. We prepared breakfast together, and found it very good fun. The housework was soon done, and when brushes and brooms and pails were quiet again, the house was still indeed. It is wonderful what a difference one makes in a house. We really missed Mrs. Dorman, quite apart from considerations concerning pots and pans. We spent the day in dusting our books and putting them straight, and dined gaily on cold steak and coffee. Laura was, if possible, brighter and gayer and sweeter than usual, and I began to think that a little domestic toil was really good for her. We had never been so merry since we were married, and the walk we had that afternoon was, I think, the happiest time of all my life. When we had watched the deep scarlet clouds slowly pale into leaden grey against a pale-green sky, and saw the white mists curl up along the hedgerows in the distant marsh, we came back to the house, silently, hand in hand.

"You are sad, my darling," I said, half-jestingly, as we sat down together in our little parlour. I expected a disclaimer, for my own silence had been the silence of complete happiness. To my surprise she said—

"Yes. I think I am sad, or rather I am uneasy. I don't think I'm very well. I have shivered three or four times since we came in, and it is not cold, is it?"

"No," I said, and hoped it was not a chill caught from the treacherous mists that roll up from the marshes in the dying light. No—she said, she did not think so. Then, after a silence, she spoke suddenly—

"Do you ever have presentiments of evil?"

"No," I said, smiling, "and I shouldn't believe in them if I had."

"I do," she went on; "the night my father died I knew it, though he was right away in the north of Scotland." I did not answer in words.

She sat looking at the fire for some time in silence, gently stroking my hand. At last she sprang up, came behind me, and, drawing my head back, kissed me.

"There, it's over now," she said. "What a baby I am! Come, light the candles, and we'll have some of these new Rubinstein duets."

And we spent a happy hour or two at the piano.

At about half-past ten I began to long for the good-night pipe, but Laura looked so white that I felt it would be brutal of me to fill our sitting-room with the fumes of strong cavendish.

"I'll take my pipe outside," I said.

"Let me come, too."

"No, sweetheart, not to-night; you're much too tired. I shan't be long. Get to bed, or I shall have an invalid to nurse to-morrow as well as the boots to clean."

I kissed her and was turning to go, when she flung her arms round my neck, and held me as if she would never let me go again. I stroked her hair.

"Come, Pussy, you're over-tired. The housework has been too much for you."

She loosened her clasp a little and drew a deep breath.

"No. We've been very happy to-day, Jack, haven't we? Don't stay out too long."

"I won't, my dearie."

I strolled out of the front door, leaving it unlatched. What a night it was! The jagged masses of heavy dark cloud were rolling at intervals from horizon to horizon, and thin white wreaths covered the stars. Through all the rush of the cloud river, the moon swam, breasting the waves and disappearing again in the darkness. When now and again her light reached the woodlands they seemed to be slowly and noiselessly waving in time to the swing of the clouds above them. There was a strange grey light over all the earth; the fields had that shadowy bloom over them which only comes from the marriage of dew and moonshine, or frost and starlight.

I walked up and down, drinking in the beauty of the quiet earth and the changing sky. The night was absolutely silent. Nothing seemed to be abroad. There was no skurrying of rabbits, or twitter of the half-asleep birds. And though the clouds went sailing across the sky, the wind that drove them never came low enough to rustle the dead leaves in the woodland paths. Across the meadows I could see the church tower standing out black and grey against the sky. I walked there thinking over our three months of happiness—and of my wife, her dear eyes, her loving ways. Oh, my little girl! my own little girl; what a vision came then of a long, glad life for you and me together!

I heard a bell-beat from the church. Eleven already! I turned to go in, but the night held me. I could not go back into our little warm rooms yet. I would go up to the church. I felt vaguely that it would be good to carry my love and thankfulness to the sanctuary whither so many loads of sorrow and gladness had been borne by the men and women of the dead years.

I looked in at the low window as I went by. Laura was half lying on her chair in front of the fire. I could not see her face, only her little head showed dark against the pale blue wall. She was quite still. Asleep, no doubt. My heart reached out to her, as I went on. There must be a God, I thought, and a God who was good. How otherwise could anything so sweet and dear as she have ever been imagined?

I walked slowly along the edge of the wood. A sound broke the stillness of the night, it was a rustling in the wood. I stopped and listened. The sound stopped too. I went on, and now distinctly heard another step than mine answer mine like an echo. It was a poacher or a wood-stealer, most likely, for these were not unknown in our Arcadian neighbourhood. But whoever it was, he was a fool not to step more lightly. I turned into the wood, and now the footstep seemed to come from the path I had just left. It must be an echo, I thought. The wood looked perfect in the moonlight. The large dying ferns and the brushwood showed where through thinning foliage the pale light came down. The tree trunks stood up like Gothic columns all around me. They reminded me of the church, and I turned into the bier-balk, and passed through the corpse-gate between the graves to the low porch. I paused for a moment on the stone seat where Laura and I had watched the fading landscape. Then I noticed that the door of the church was open, and I blamed myself for having left it unlatched the other night. We were the only people who ever cared to come to the church except on Sundays, and I was vexed to think that through our carelessness the damp autumn airs had had a chance of getting in and injuring the old fabric. I went in. It will seem strange, perhaps, that I should have gone half-way up the aisle before I remembered—with a sudden chill, followed by as sudden a rush of self-contempt—that this was the very day and hour when, according to tradition, the "shapes drawed out man-size in marble" began to walk.

Having thus remembered the legend, and remembered it with a shiver, of which I was ashamed, I could not do otherwise than walk up towards the altar, just to look at the figures—as I said to myself; really what I wanted was to assure myself, first, that I did not believe the legend, and, secondly, that it was not true. I was rather glad that I had come. I thought now I could tell Mrs. Dorman how vain her fancies were, and how peacefully the marble figures slept on through the ghastly hour. With my hands in my pockets I passed up the aisle. In the grey dim light the eastern end of the church looked larger than usual, and the arches above the two tombs looked larger too. The moon came out and showed me the reason. I stopped short, my heart gave a leap that nearly choked me, and then sank sickeningly.

The "bodies drawed out man-size" *were gone*, and their marble slabs lay wide and bare in the vague moonlight that slanted through the east window.

Were they really gone? or was I mad? Clenching my nerves, I stooped and passed my hand over the smooth slabs, and felt their flat unbroken surface. Had some one taken the things away? Was it some vile practical joke? I would make sure, anyway. In an instant I had made a torch of a newspaper, which happened to be in my pocket, and lighting it held it high above my head. Its yellow glare illumined the dark arches and those slabs. The figures *were* gone. And I was alone in the church; or was I alone?

And then a horror seized me, a horror indefinable and indescribable—an overwhelming certainty of supreme and accomplished calamity. I flung down the torch and tore along the aisle and out through the porch, biting my lips as I ran to keep myself from shrieking aloud. Oh, was I mad—or what was this that possessed me? I leaped the churchyard wall and took the straight cut across the fields, led by the light from our windows. Just as I got over the first stile, a dark figure seemed to spring out of the ground. Mad still with that certainty of misfortune, I made for the thing that stood in my path, shouting, "Get out of the way, can't you!"

But my push met with a more vigorous resistance than I had expected. My arms were caught just above the elbow and held as in a vice, and the raw-boned Irish doctor actually shook me.

"Would ye?" he cried, in his own unmistakable accents—"would ye, then?"

"Let me go, you fool," I gasped. "The marble figures have gone from the church; I tell you they've gone."

He broke into a ringing laugh. "I'll have to give ye a draught to-morrow, I see. Ye've bin smoking too much and listening to old wives' tales."

"I tell you, I've seen the bare slabs."

"Well, come back with me. I'm going up to old Palmer's—his daughter's ill; we'll look in at the church and let me see the bare slabs."

"You go, if you like," I said, a little less frantic for his laughter; "I'm going home to my wife."

"Rubbish, man," said he; "d'ye think I'll permit of that? Are ye to go saying all yer life that ye've seen solid marble endowed with vitality, and me to go all me life saying ye were a coward? No, sir—ye shan't do ut."

The night air—a human voice—and I think also the physical contact with this six feet of solid common sense, brought me back a little to my ordinary self, and the word "coward" was a mental shower-bath.

"Come on, then," I said sullenly; "perhaps you're right."

He still held my arm tightly. We got over the stile and back to the church. All was still as death. The place smelt very damp and earthy. We walked up the aisle. I am not ashamed to confess that I shut my eyes: I knew the figures would not be there. I heard Kelly strike a match.

"Here they are, ye see, right enough; ye've been dreaming or drinking, asking yer pardon for the imputation."

I opened my eyes. By Kelly's expiring vesta I saw two shapes lying "in their marble" on their slabs. I drew a deep breath, and caught his hand.

"I'm awfully indebted to you," I said. "It must have been some trick of light, or I have been working rather hard, perhaps that's it. Do you know, I was quite convinced they were gone."

"I'm aware of that," he answered rather grimly; "ye'll have to be careful of that brain of yours, my friend, I assure ye."

He was leaning over and looking at the right-hand figure, whose stony face was the most villainous and deadly in expression.

"By Jove," he said, "something has been afoot here—this hand is broken."

And so it was. I was certain that it had been perfect the last time Laura and I had been there.

"Perhaps some one has *tried* to remove them," said the young doctor.

"That won't account for my impression," I objected.

"Too much painting and tobacco will account for that, well enough."

"Come along," I said, "or my wife will be getting anxious. You'll come in and have a drop of whisky and drink confusion to ghosts and better sense to me."

"I ought to go up to Palmer's, but it's so late now I'd best leave it till the morning," he replied. "I was kept late at the Union, and I've had to see a lot of people since. All right, I'll come back with ye."

I think he fancied I needed him more than did Palmer's girl, so, discussing how such an illusion could have been possible, and deducing from this experience large generalities concerning ghostly apparitions, we walked up to our cottage. We saw, as we walked up the garden-path, that bright light streamed out of the front door, and presently saw that the parlour door was open too. Had she gone out?

"Come in," I said, and Dr. Kelly followed me into the parlour. It was all ablaze with candles, not only the wax ones, but at least a dozen guttering, glaring tallow dips, stuck in vases and ornaments in unlikely places. Light, I knew, was Laura's remedy for nervousness. Poor child! Why had I left her? Brute that I was.

We glanced round the room, and at first we did not see her. The window was open, and the draught set all the candles flaring one way. Her chair was empty and her handkerchief and book lay on the floor. I turned to the window. There, in the recess of the window, I saw her. Oh, my child, my love, had she gone to that window to watch for me? And what had come into the room behind her? To what had she turned with that look of frantic fear and horror? Oh, my little one, had she thought that it was I whose step she heard, and turned to meet—what?

She had fallen back across a table in the window, and her body lay half on it and half on the window-seat, and her head hung down over the table, the brown hair loosened and fallen to the carpet. Her lips were drawn back, and her eyes wide, wide open. They saw nothing now. What had they seen last?

The doctor moved towards her, but I pushed him aside and sprang to her; caught her in my arms and cried—

"It's all right, Laura! I've got you safe, wifie."

She fell into my arms in a heap. I clasped her and kissed her, and called her by all her pet names, but I think I knew all the time that she was dead. Her hands were tightly clenched. In one of them she held something fast. When I was quite sure that she was dead, and that nothing mattered at all any more, I let him open her hand to see what she held.

It was a grey marble finger.

The Mass for the Dead

I was awake—widely, cruelly awake. I had been awake all night; what sleep could there be for me when the woman I loved was to be married next morning—married, and not to me?

I went to my room early; the family party in the drawing-room maddened me. Grouped about the round table with the stamped plush cover, each was busy with work, or book, or newspaper, but not too busy to stab my heart through and through with their talk of the wedding.

Her people were near neighbours of mine, so why should her marriage not be canvassed in my home circle?

They did not mean to be cruel; they did not know that I loved her; but she knew it. I told her, but she knew it before that. She knew it from the moment when I came back from three years of musical study in Germany—came back and met her in the wood where we used to go nutting when we were children.

I looked into her eyes, and my whole soul trembled with thankfulness that I was living in a world that held her also. I turned and walked by her side, through the tangled green wood, and we talked of the long-ago days, and it was, "Have you forgotten?" and "Do you remember?" till we reached her garden gate. Then I said—

"Good-bye; no, *auf wiedersehn*, and in a very little time, I hope."

And she answered—

"Good-bye. By the way, you haven't congratulated me yet."

"Congratulated you?"

"Yes, did I not tell you I am to marry Mr. Benoliel next month?"

And she turned away, and went up the garden slowly.

I asked my people, and they said it was true. Kate, my dear playfellow, was to marry this Spaniard, rich, wilful, accustomed to win, polished in manners and base in life. Why was she to marry him?

"No one knows," said my father, "but her father is talked about in the city, and Benoliel, the Spaniard, is rich. Perhaps that's it."

That was it. She told me so when, after two weeks spent with her and near her, I implored her to break so vile a chain and to come to me, who loved her—whom she loved.

"You are quite right," she said calmly. We were sitting in the window-seat of the oak parlour in her father's desolate old house. "I do love you, and I shall marry Mr. Benoliel."

"Why?"

"Look around you and ask me why, if you can."

I looked around—on the shabby, bare room, with its faded hangings of sage-green moreen, its threadbare carpet, its patched, washed-out chintz chair-covers. I looked out through the square, latticed window at the ragged, unkempt lawn, at her own gown—of poor material, though she wore it as queens might desire to wear ermine—and I understood.

Kate is obstinate; it is her one fault; I knew how vain would be my entreaties, yet I offered them; how unavailing my arguments, yet they were set forth; how useless my love and my sorrow, yet I showed them to her.

"No," she answered, but she flung her arms round my neck as she spoke, and held me as one may hold one's best treasure. "No, no; you are poor, and he is rich. You wouldn't have me break my father's heart: he's so proud, and if he doesn't get some money next month, he will be ruined. I'm not deceiving any one. Mr. Benoliel knows I don't care for him; and if I marry him, he is going to advance my father a large sum of money. Oh, I assure you that everything has been talked over and settled. There is no going from it."

"Child! child!" I cried, "how calmly you speak of it! Don't you see that you are selling your soul and throwing mine away?"

"Father Fabian says I am doing right," she answered, unclasping her hands, but holding mine in them, and looking at me with those clear, grey eyes of hers. "Are we to be unselfish in everything else, and in love to think only of our own happiness? I love you, and I shall marry him. Would you rather the positions were reversed?"

"Yes," I said, "for then I would make you love me."

"Perhaps *he* will," she said bitterly. Even in that moment her mouth trembled with the ghost of a smile. She always loved to tease. She goes through more moods in a day than most other women in a year. Drowning the smile came tears, but she controlled them, and she said—

"Good-bye; you see I am right, don't you? Oh, Jasper, I wish I hadn't told you I loved you. It will only make you more unhappy."

"It makes my one happiness," I answered; "nothing can take that from me. And that happiness *he* will never have. Say again that you love me!"

"I love you! I love you! I love you!"

With further folly of tears and mad loving words we parted, and I bore my heartache away, leaving her to bear hers into her new life.

And now she was to be married to-morrow, and I could not sleep.

When the darkness became unbearable I lighted a candle, and then lay staring vacantly at the roses on the wall-paper, or following with my eyes the lines and curves of the heavy mahogany furniture.

The solidity of my surroundings oppressed me. In the dull light the wardrobe loomed like a hearse, and my violin case looked like a child's coffin.

I reached a book and read till my eyes ached and the letters danced a *pas fantastique* up and down the page.

I got up and had ten minutes with the dumbbells. I sponged my face and hands with cold water and tried again to sleep—vainly. I lay there, miserably wide awake.

I tried to say poetry, the half-forgotten tasks of my school days even, but through everything ran the refrain—

"Kate is to be married to-morrow, and not to me, not to me!"

I tried counting up to a thousand. I tried to imagine sheep in a lane, and to count them as they jumped through a gap in an imaginary hedge—all the time-honoured spells with which sleep is wooed—vainly.

Then the Waits came, and a torture to the nerves was superadded to the torture of the heart. After fifteen minutes of carols every fibre of me seemed vibrating in an agony of physical misery.

To banish the echo of "The Mistletoe Bough," I hummed softly to myself a melody of Palestrina's, and felt more awake than ever.

Then the thing happened which nothing will ever explain. As I lay there I heard, breaking through and gradually overpowering the air I was suggesting, a harmony which I had never heard before, beautiful beyond description, and as distinct and definite as any song man's ears have ever listened to.

My first half-formed thought was, "more Waits," but the music was choral music, true and sweet; with it mingled an organ's notes, and with every note the music grew in volume. It is absurd to suggest that I dreamed it, for, still hearing the music, I leaped out of bed and opened the window. The music grew fainter. There was no one to be seen in the snowy garden below. Shivering, I shut the window. The music grew more distinct, and I became aware that I was listening to a mass—a funeral mass, and one which I had never heard before. I lay in my bed and followed the whole course of the office.

The music ceased.

I was sitting up in bed, my candle alight, and myself as wide awake as ever, and more than ever possessed by the thought of *her*.

But with a difference. Before, I had only mourned the loss of her: now, my thoughts of her were mingled with an indescribable dread. The sense of death and decay that had come to me with that strange, beautiful music, coloured all my thoughts. I was filled with fancies of hushed houses, black garments, rooms where white flowers and white linen lay in a deathly stillness. I heard echoes of tears, and of dim-voiced bells tolling monotonously. I shivered, as it were on the brink of irreparable woe, and in its contemplation I watched the dull dawn slowly overcome the pale flame of my candle, now burnt down into its socket.

I felt that I must see Kate once again before she gave herself away. Before ten o'clock I was in the oak parlour. She came to me. As she entered the room, her pallor, her swollen eyelids and the misery in her eyes wrung my heart as even that night of agony had not done. I literally could not speak. I held out my hands.

Would she reproach me for coming to her again, for forcing upon her a second time the anguish of parting?

She did not. She laid her hands in mine, and said—

"I am thankful you have come; do you know, I think I am going mad? Don't let me go mad, Jasper."

The look in her eyes underlined her words.

I stammered something and kissed her hands. I was with her again, and joy fought again with grief.

"I must tell some one. If I am mad, don't lock me up. Take care of me, won't you?"

Would I not?

"Understand," she went on, "it was not a dream. I was wide awake, thinking of you. The Waits had not long gone, and I—I was looking at your likeness. I was not asleep."

I shivered as I held her fast.

"As Heaven sees us, I did not dream it. I heard a mass sung, and, Jasper, it was a mass for the dead. I followed the office. You are not a Catholic, but I thought—I feared—oh, I don't know what I thought. I am thankful there is nothing wrong with you."

I felt a sudden certainty, and complete sense of power possess me. Now, in this her moment of weakness, while she was so completely under the influence of a strong emotion, I could and would save her from Benoliel, and myself from life-long pain.

"Kate," I said, "I believe it is a warning. You shall not marry this man. You shall marry me, and none other."

She leaned her head against my shoulder; she seemed to have forgotten her father and all the reasons for her marriage with Benoliel.

"You don't think I'm mad? No? Then take care of me; take me away; I feel safe with you."

Thus all obstacles vanished in less time than the length of a lover's kiss. I dared not stop to consider the coincidence of supernatural warning—nor what it might mean. Face to face with crowned hope, I am proud to remember that common sense held her own. The room in which we were had a French window. I fetched her garden hat and a shawl from the hall, and we went out through the still, white garden. We did not meet a soul. When we reached my father's garden I took her in by the back way, to the summer-house, and left her, though I was half afraid to leave her, while I went into the house. I snatched my violin and cheque book, took all my spare money, scrawled a line to my father and rejoined her.

Still no one had seen us.

We walked to a station five miles away; and by the time Benoliel would reach the church, I was leaving Doctors' Commons with a special licence in my pocket. Two hours later Kate was my wife, and we were quietly and prosaically eating our wedding-breakfast in the dining-room of the Grand Hotel.

"And where shall we go?" I said.

"I don't know," she answered, smiling; "you have not much money, have you?"

"Oh dear me, yes. I'm not rich, but I'm not absolutely a church mouse."

"Could we go to Devonshire?" she asked, twisting her new ring round and round.

"Devonshire! Why, that is where—"

"Yes, I know: Benoliel arranged to go there. Jasper, I am afraid of Benoliel."

"Then why—"

"Foolish person," she answered. "Do you think that Benoliel will be likely to go to Devonshire *now*?"

We went to Devonshire—I had had a small legacy a few months earlier, and I did not permit money cares to trouble my new and beautiful happiness. My only fear was that she would be saddened by thoughts of her father; but I am thankful to remember that in those first days she, too, was happy—so happy that there seemed to be hardly room in her mind for any thought but of me. And every hour of every day I said to my soul—

"But for that portent, whatever it boded, she might have been not my wife but his."

The first four or five days of our marriage are flowers that memory keeps always fresh. Kate's face had recovered its wild-rose bloom, and she laughed and sang and jested and enjoyed all our little daily adventures with the fullest, freest-hearted gaiety. Then I committed the supreme imbecility of my life—one of those acts of folly on which one looks back all one's life with a half stamp of the foot, and the unanswerable question, "How on earth could I have been such a fool?"

We were sitting in a little sitting-room, hideous in intention, but redeemed by blazing fire and the fact that two were there, sitting hand-in-hand, gazing into the fire and talking of their future and of their love. There was nothing to trouble us; no one had discovered our whereabouts, and my wife's fear of Benoliel's revenge seemed to have dissolved before the flame of our happiness.

And as we sat there, peaceful and untroubled, the Imp of the Perverse jogged my elbow, as, alas! he does so often, and I was moved to tell my wife that I, too, had heard that unearthly midnight music—that her hearing of it was not, as she had grown to think, a mere nightmare—a strange dream—but something more strange, more significant. I told her how I had heard the mass for the dead, and all the tale of that night. She listened silently, and I thought her strangely indifferent. When I had finished, she took her hand from mine and covered her face.

"I believe it was a warning to us to flee temptation. We ought never to have married. Oh, my poor father!"

Her tone was one that I had never heard before. Its hopeless misery appalled me. And justly. For no arguments, no entreaties, no caresses, could win my wife back to the mood of an hour before.

She tried to be cheerful, but her gaiety was forced, and her laughter stung my heart.

She spoke no more about the music, and when I tried to reason with her about it she smiled a gloomy little smile, and said—

"I cannot be happy. I will not be happy. It is wrong. I have been very selfish and wicked. You think me very idiotic, I know, but I believe there is a curse on us. We shall never be happy again."

"Don't you love me any more?" I asked like a fool.

"Love you?" She only repeated my words, but I was satisfied on that score. But those were miserable days. We loved each other passionately, yet our hours were spent like those of lovers on the eve of parting. Long, long silences took the place of foolish little jokes and childish talk which happy lovers know. And more than once, waking in the night, I heard my wife sobbing, and feigned sleep, with the bitter knowledge that I had no power to comfort her. I knew that the thought of her father was with her always, and that her anxiety about him grew, day by day. I wore myself out in trying to think of some way to divert her thoughts from him. I could not, indeed, pay his debts, but I could have him to live with us, a much greater sacrifice; and having a good connection, both as a musician and composer, I did not doubt that I could support her and him in comfort.

But Kate had made up her mind that the disgrace of bankruptcy would break her father's heart; and my Kate is not easy to convince or persuade.

At Torquay it occurred to me that perhaps it would be well for her to see a priest. True, Father Fabian had counselled her to marry Benoliel, but I could hardly believe that most priests would advise a girl to marry a bad man, whom she did not love, for the sake of any worldly gain whatsoever.

She received the suggestion with favour, but without enthusiasm, and we sought out a Catholic church to make inquiries. As we opened the outer door of the church we heard music, and as we stood in the entrance and I laid my hand on the heavy inner door, my other hand was caught by Kate.

"Jasper," she whispered, "it is the same!"

Some person opening the door behind us compelled us to move forward. In another moment we stood in the dusky church—stood hand-in-hand in dim daylight, listening to the same music that each had heard in the lonely night on the eve of our wedding.

I put my arm round my wife and drew her back.

"Come away, my darling," I whispered; "it is a funeral service."

She turned her eyes on me. "I *must* understand, I must see who it is. I shall go mad if you take me away now. I cannot bear any more."

We walked up the aisle, and placed ourselves as near as possible to the spot where the coffin lay, covered with flowers and with tapers burning about it. And we heard that music again, every note of it the same that each had heard before. And when the service was over I whispered to the sacristan—

"Whose music was that?"

"Our organist's," he answered; "it is the first time they've had it. Fine, wasn't it?"

"Who is the—who was—who is being buried?"

"A foreign gentleman, sir; they do say as his lady as was to be gave him the slip on his wedding day, and he'd given her father thousands they say, if the truth was known."

"But what was he doing here?"

"Well, that's the curious part, sir. To show his independence, what does he do but go the same tour he'd planned for his wedding trip. And there was a railway accident, and him and every one in his carriage killed in a twinkling, so to speak. Lucky for the young lady she was off with somebody else."

The sacristan laughed softly to himself.

Kate's fingers gripped my arm.

"What was his name?" she asked.

I would not have asked: I did not wish to hear it.

"Benoliel," said the sacristan. "Curious name and curious tale. Every one's talking of it."

Every one had something else to talk of when it was found that Benoliel's pride, which had permitted him to buy a wife, had shrunk from reclaiming the purchase money when the purchase was lost to him. And to the man who had been willing to sell his daughter, the retention of her price seemed perfectly natural.

From the moment when she heard Benoliel's name on the sacristan's lips, all Kate's gaiety and happiness returned. She loved me, and she hated Benoliel. She was married to me, and he was dead; and his death was far more of a shock to me than to her. Women are curiously kind and curiously cruel. And she never could see why her father should not have kept the money. It is noteworthy that women, even the cleverest and the best of them, have no perception of what men mean by honour.

How do I account for the music? My good critic, my business is to tell my story—not to account for it.

And do I not pity Benoliel? Yes. I can afford, now, to pity most men, alive or dead.

THE END

A Note About the Author

Edith Nesbit (1858–1924) was an English writer of children's literature. Born in Kennington, Nesbit was raised by her mother following the death of her father—a prominent chemist—when she was only four years old. Due to her sister Mary's struggle with tuberculosis, the family travelled throughout England, France, Spain, and Germany for years. After Mary passed, Edith and her mother returned to England for good, eventually settling in London where, at eighteen, Edith met her future husband, a bank clerk named Hubert Bland. The two—who became prominent socialists and were founding members of the Fabian Society—had a famously difficult marriage, and both had numerous affairs. Nesbit began her career as a poet, eventually turning to children's literature and publishing around forty novels, story collections, and picture books. A contemporary of such figures of Lewis Carroll and Kenneth Grahame, Nesbit was notable as a writer who pioneered the children's adventure story in fiction. Among her most popular works are *The Railway Children* (1906) and *The Story of the Amulet* (1906), the former of which was adapted into a 1970 film, and the latter of which served as a profound influence on C.S. Lewis' Narnia series. A friend and mentor to George Bernard Shaw and H.G. Wells, Nesbit's work has inspired and entertained generations of children and adults, including such authors as J.K. Rowling, Noël Coward, and P.L. Travers.

A Note from the Publisher

Spanning many genres, from non-fiction essays to literature classics to children's books and lyric poetry, Mint Edition books showcase the master works of our time in a modern new package. The text is freshly typeset, is clean and easy to read, and features a new note about the author in each volume. Many books also include exclusive new introductory material. Every book boasts a striking new cover, which makes it as appropriate for collecting as it is for gift giving. Mint Edition books are only printed when a reader orders them, so natural resources are not wasted. We're proud that our books are never manufactured in excess and exist only in the exact quantity they need to be read and enjoyed.

Discover more of your favorite classics with Bookfinity™.

- Track your reading with custom book lists.
- Get great book recommendations for your personalized Reader Type.
- Add reviews for your favorite books.
- AND MUCH MORE!

Visit **bookfinity.com** and take the fun Reader Type quiz to get started.

Enjoy our classic and modern companion pairings!